A DANCE FOR SURVIVAL . . .

Lovely young Fiona was well-bred and intelligent, yet without her job as dancing hostess at the tawdry nightclub, she would have starved. For it was the beginning of the Depression and her father had died suddenly, leaving her penniless.

The hours were long and her feet often felt as though they might never move again. But her plucky spirit, her naive courage kept her going through the most difficult days . . . until the lecherous Lord Winthrop set his cap for her. And if she said no, the rich nobleman would surely see that she lost her job.

But if she said yes, could she live with herself . . . or with the handsome, captivating bachelor, with whom she'd fallen desperately in love?

Pyramid Books

by

BARBARA CARTLAND

DANCE
ON MY
HEART

Barbara Cartland

PYRAMID BOOKS ▲ NEW YORK

DANCE ON MY HEART

A PYRAMID BOOK

Pyramid edition published January 1977

Printed in the United States of America

Pyramid Books are published by Pyramid Publications (Harcourt Brace Jovanovich, Inc.). Its trademarks, consisting of the word "Pyramid" and the portrayal of a pyramid, are registered in the United States Patent Office.

PYRAMID PUBLICATIONS (Harcourt Brace Jovanovich, Inc.). 757 Third Avenue, New York, N.Y. 10017

AUTHOR'S NOTE

I wrote this book at the end of the 1920's. There was vast unemployment over the whole of Great Britain. Jobs were almost unobtainable. This story of Fiona is a true history of the times only many did not end so happily.

DANCE ON MY HEART

CHAPTER ONE

1920

The Rolls Royce had its bonnet open and its engine running.

The chauffeur, as he cleaned it, was whistling the latest tune, with which, only a few weeks old, London was already satiated.

Children were playing in the early morning sunshine on the cobble-stones of the mews.

Fiona stirred in her narrow bed, and finally awoke.

She lay for a few minutes trying to recapture her dreams, but gradually full consciousness of the noise outside her window roused her to complete wakefulness.

"What a row," she thought resentfully, wondering if she could find as cheap a room in some quieter spot.

The room, which was just large enough to hold a narrow iron bedstead, a chest of drawers and a washing-stand, was only desirable from the point of view of its price.

Ten shillings a week was what Fiona paid regularly to the chauffeur's wife who was her landlady, and she had found that hard enough until last night, when she had started on a new job with the magnificent salary of thirty-five shillings a week.

Remembrance of this new job came back to her now when she realised, as she opened them, how much her eyes smarted from the smoky atmosphere she had left barely five hours ago.

Her legs were tired and her feet sore.

The new shoes bought for the occasion had been stiff and a trifle tight, and this morning her feet were achingly resentful of the fact.

Yet it was with complacent pleasure that she thought of her triumph in securing the job over the heads of many other applicants.

They had all been struggling with that hungry look in their eyes for anything which would keep them from penury.

The job itself, in its full glory, was known as "dance-hostess," at the most fashionable restaurant in the West End.

Paglioni's was frequented by Society and patronised by the younger Royalties. It employed two girls termed "dance-hostesses," and a man who enjoyed the same standing.

Their duties were to dance the moment the band began at ten o'clock, so as to encourage other people on to the floor.

They sat at a table, and any partnerless male could be introduced to the "dance-hostesses," while the man sought out elderly women whose husbands were too old or too apathetic to learn the latest steps.

It was all intensely respectable.

A man wishing to dance with one of the "hostesses" would approach either Paglioni himself, or send a message by a waiter that he wished to speak to their male companion.

He was then formally introduced, and the "hostess" would accept his invitation to dance.

At most restaurants, tips were expected and given by the partners, but then the salary was only ten shillings a week—a purely nominal "retaining fee."

Paglioni, however, had an idea that it encouraged more men to dine singly at his restaurant if they could dance with a girl and not have to pay her. He impressed his magnificence on his patrons, informing them that the girls received large salaries.

Occasionally a man would be so pleased with his partner that he would slip a ten-shilling note into her hand on leaving, or a stranger would not know the rule of the house.

It was a disadvantage to the girls, although it benefited Paglioni.

Many men would desert their clubs for the restaurant, knowing that if they felt shy alone they could get a "hostess" to join them for the cost of an extra drink.

Last night Fiona had found that, of her many partners, none of them would see sixty again.

What was surprising was that most of them danced well, of which in most cases they were boastfully conceited.

At nine-thirty Fiona and her companions had to be at their post. They were expected to be well dressed, and Paglioni had informed her that one dress would not be sufficient.

"There must be a change," he had said, in an airy way, as if evening dresses were easily procured on the princely sum he paid them.

But Fiona had been too thankful to get the job to worry at that moment, whatever conditions he imposed.

"The one thing for you to remember," he had said in broken English, "is that you are here to please my clients. That is the most important thing. The client must be pleased. If you do not please them, you go. And I do not give any notice."

Fiona had remembered his words as she journeyed up Piccadilly in a bus.

She had not worried about her appearance. She knew that her red chiffon dress, bought cheaply in the sales, was all right, and became her.

She had already made a hole in her week's earnings to buy the red shoes to match, and a little beaded evening bag, feeling that her serviceable black leather one was hardly in keeping.

11

Her hair had been waved, her nails manicured, and she was fully conscious that the other occupants of the bus stared at her in admiration.

She had no evening coat, but the black cloth one which she wore in the daytime was warm, and could be quickly discarded in the cloakroom.

"I must keep this job," she thought to herself. "Even if the pay is small, I at least get one good meal a day."

Paglioni provided supper—exclusive of drinks, of course.

She was early, and had to wait in the lounge for the other two to appear.

Clare Bailey was tall and dark, and Fiona realised at once that Paglioni had chosen her because they were such opposite types.

Fiona's fair hair, blue eyes and very English appearance were a delightful foil for Clare's sinuousness and dark, almost Oriental beauty.

She had been at Paglioni's for two months, and had proved herself a success with the clientele.

She had lovely clothes, which filled Fiona with envy, until she discovered that Clare had managed to get a well-known dressmaker to allow her to borrow her models.

Clare's one horror was that a dress might be spoilt, in which case she would have to pay for it.

"Men are so rough," she confided to Fiona.

Her smirk as she said it made Fiona uneasily apprehensive of what she herself might have to experience later.

Paul, the professional "host," was, as might be expected, tall, dark and good-looking. He had tried for some time to be a shop-walker, but had been sacked from several places for incompetence, due entirely to his innate laziness.

He could not get up in the morning, and found long hours of standing about too irksome to be endured. He therefore enjoyed his present position, which enabled him to spend most of the day in bed.

He made more than the girls, by giving dancing-lessons but as they were generally only a subterfuge for the elderly ladies to pursue a closer acquaintance with him, he was not required to put in an appearance until after luncheon at the earliest.

Then he would present himself at their houses, to glide for an hour with them on their parquet floors, before indulging in tea and a little chat about himself.

It was also suspected that he insisted on getting tips in spite of Paglioni's rule, not dancing twice unless compelled with a woman who forgot.

Being a man, he had the privilege of asking, while the girls were powerless to refuse an invitation.

He had been at the restaurant a long time, and Paglioni well knew his worth, for his female admirers came regularly for dinner and supper, bringing their non-dancing husbands to pay the bill.

Paul had been condescendingly polite to Fiona. He had the rather suave, over-polished manners of a gigolo, which he did not drop in his conversation with the girls, at any rate not within the precincts of Paglioni's lounge.

When they were seated at their table, and the band, after shuffling into their seats, started with the bright tune which was to raise the atmosphere to one of gaiety, he turned to Fiona with a little bow.

"Will you dance this with me, Miss Mayne?" he said.

Inwardly nervous but outwardly composed, Fiona rose.

She was terrified of making a mistake, but Paul was a very good dancer.

Although they danced for quite three minutes alone, before they were joined by three or four other couples, she managed to look as if she were accustomed to giving such an exhibition.

"We can now go back to our food," Paul said at last, as at least six couples were dancing gaily, and others seemed to be preparing to join them.

They went back to their table, to find that the fish which had been given them for supper was cold.

But it was still appetising to anyone who had lived

13

on the scraps which Fiona had had for the last few weeks while she was looking for a job.

London was full of people seeking positions, regardless of the smallness of the salaries offered. Anything to be in work, to feel some sort of security against that terrible dread of starvation.

Fiona's father had been a solicitor in a London suburb where she had lived all her life.

He had been a morose, dour man, who had accepted life and death with a gloomy fatality which had made him no friends, and rendered Fiona's childhood a lengthy passage of loneliness.

Her mother had died when she was young, and there had been no one to take her place.

The house was managed by a single servant, who had no affection either for her father or for herself, but who did her work passably well.

Fiona was sent to the local High School, where she received an education which fitted her for no particular job, but showed her that a post of schoolmistress or governess was entirely out of the question.

When she left school, she could type somewhat laboriously; but too slow to be employed anywhere but in her father's office.

Here she managed to be helpful for two years, receiving no wages and more grumbling than thanks.

Six months ago her father had died very suddenly.

When his affairs were cleared up, Fiona found herself with a capital of one hundred pounds. Her father was not a popular man, and his business was a poor one.

The house, which she did not want, was luckily nearly at the end of a long lease, and when she explained her plight to the landlord he generously offered to relieve her of her last year's tenancy.

She quickly realised there was no likelihood of her obtaining work locally.

The market was already glutted with girls wanting to be independent, or really in need of employment, and with her hundred pounds she had come to London and searched the West End.

She was persuaded by her bank manager to invest the hundred pounds in War Loan, and she made a vow to herself that if possible she would not draw it out, unless in really desperate straits.

Once that money was gone, there was nothing and nobody between her and starvation.

Her mother had come from the West Country, but Fiona had never met or heard of any of her relations, although she presumed vaguely that there were some still living.

Her father had been born in the North, and so far as she knew he had no relations; his death seemed to be unmourned by any friends.

To begin with, Fiona had to find herself a room, and her mews lodging, near Marble Arch underground station, was the first which caught her eye.

She had taken it, until she could find, or her salary permitted, something better.

She did her own room, but her landlady provided her with breakfast.

Tea, none too hot and far too strong, and bread and margarine, were placed outside her room somewhere about ten o'clock every morning. If she woke later, and the tea was cold, that was her fault.

She had stipulated on this arrangement from the moment she decided that a restaurant or night-club life was the best thing for her.

The first week she had sought a job as mannequin or saleswoman in the better-class shops, only to find that one question stood in her way unsurmountably:

"Have you had any experience?"

For the saleswomen it was the same, and there were queues of applicants for every vacancy.

It was an advertisement in one of the papers which made Fiona apply for a job as "dance-hostess".

She had not obtained that particular job, but she had realised that such employment was open to a pretty, well-dressed girl.

She knew that she was smart at the moment, for her clothes were new. In mourning for her father she knew

15

that their sombre black showed up her fairness to its best advantage.

She had wandered, therefore, from cabaret to night club, and from night club to restaurant, meeting so often the same girls that one or two of them began to smile and chat with her.

She was amazed at their good-humored acceptance of refusal, but some of them seemed too numb to protest or even swear at the fate which sent them away.

The others would shrug their shoulders, or joke about their ill-fortune.

It was after she had been refused admission, for the post was filled, at a rather low night club in Regent Street, that she heard Paglioni was likely to require another "hostess."

"Brenda's got a job on the stage," the girl next to her was saying. "They go on tour next week—a try-out, I think—and if it's a success they'll come back to London. She's lucky, isn't she—four pounds a week! And that means Paglioni will be looking out for someone else.

So Fiona joined the queue which waited outside Paglioni's next morning.

It was a damp day, with a thin drizzle of rain, and they stood shivering outside for a good hour after the appointed time, before Paglioni arrived at the restaurant.

Waiters were tidying up, trying to ventilate the room from the thick haze of stale smoke. The floor was littered with ash, cigarette ends and pieces of paper.

The whole place had a tawdry, rather dirty air in the daylight, which clever lighting would conceal later on.

The moment Fiona saw Paglioni, she took an instinctive dislike to him. A thick-set, swarthy Italian, unshaven at this hour in the morning, but already smoking a cigar.

With his hat on his head, he beckoned to the girls, taking them six at a time, and they stood miserably in the centre of the floor, while he cursed a waiter for some fault his quick eyes had detected on entering.

Finally, he attended to them. Fiona, having risen

very early, was in the first six. He looked her up and down, asking her questions, and inspecting the others.

Two were not pretty enough for his liking, and he dismissed them curtly.

In the end, Fiona was selected, and while she rejoiced, she could hardly bear the disappointed faces of the others as they went away out into the drizzling rain, to start their search all over again.

Still, everyone for himself, and this morning Fiona could think only of the joy of not having to search for a job.

She stretched herself luxuriously in her bed, and glanced at the clock which ticked on a chair beside her.

"Half-past ten!"

She got out of bed, opened the door and brought in her breakfast tray.

The tea was quite cold, but she drank it, and ate the whole of the rather stale chunk of bread on the plate.

She wondered if she could do without luncheon, and wait for further food until her supper at Paglioni's to-night.

* * *

"Who is that?" Fiona asked Clare, as she went back to her seat, having been dancing a quarter of an hour.

She had been nearly a month at Paglioni's by this time, and knew a good many of the people by sight. With some of the men she was quite friendly.

The women, of course, ignored her. She had soon learned the difference in a man's behaviour towards her when he was alone, and when he was with a woman.

There was rather a nice young man with whom she had danced two or three times in succession one evening.

He had been very cheery, and had come over and sat at the table with Clare and herself, and had insisted on providing them with champagne.

This, of course, was noticed and greatly approved

17

of by Paglioni. The next night Fiona had seen her new friend arriving with a party of other men and three women.

"There's Harry," she had said excitedly to Clare, "I wonder if he will come over and speak to us."

But Clare had speedily disillusioned her.

"Of course not," she said sharply, "and for goodness' sake, Fiona, don't try to attract his attention like that. You mustn't bow or smile until he sees you first."

And Fiona quickly realised that Harry had no intention of seeing her at all that evening. He avoided meeting her glance in any way, but returned to Paglioni's two or three nights later, and was just as cheerful and friendly as he had been on their first acquaintance.

The man with whom Fiona had been dancing the moment before she spoke to Clare was tall and rather good-looking in an elderly way, but his face was lined and marked with the evident signs of too good living and dissipation.

He had an unpleasant way of dancing, too intimately, Fiona thought. Although he had said very little she had disliked him, and had seized the opportunity of returning to her own table as quickly as possible.

Her partner had ordered himself a bottle of champagne, and had returned to his table to consume it and some oysters.

He was evidently important, for he was given the table of honour—a sofa in a small alcove which was kept exclusively for the celebrities or Royalty who condescended to come to Paglioni's.

"That is Lord Winthrop," Clare said. "He is immensely rich, and lives in that lovely house at the corner of Park Lane."

"Winthrop House," Fiona said. "Of course I know it. I don't think I like him, much."

"I'm not surprised," Clare replied. "He is a beast. Here's my old boy coming alone. I shan't see you again tonight—I'm going to have supper with him."

She smiled, as an elderly General, bald-headed and short of breath, approached her.

They moved over to another table at the far end of the room, where she proceeded to order herself the most expensive things on the menu.

This was not only in accordance with Paglioni's instructions, for of course the hostesses were expected to encourage the clients to spend money; but Clare was naturally greedy.

Fiona was not long at her table before Lord Winthrop approached her again.

She rose to her feet unwillingly, feeling a strong inclination to refuse, but conscious that from the doorway Paglioni was watching.

Lord Winthrop danced fairly well, but held her far too tightly.

"You're very pretty, you know," he said at last.

"Thank you," Fiona replied, as coldly as she dared.

She did not care for compliments of this sort, anyway not from someone she disliked.

"Will you have supper with me to-morrow night?" Lord Winthrop continued.

Fiona sought wildly for an excuse.

"No," Fiona replied, "I'm so tired when I leave here, I'm only too thankful to go straight home. I think this is the end of the dance. Don't you want to go back to your supper?"

"I'll come over and dance with you later," he promised, giving her a final squeeze which sent Fiona back to her table with burning cheeks and angry eyes.

"The old fool's getting fresh," she told Paul.

He laughed.

"I shouldn't mind," he said, "after all, he's rich enough."

"I think he's revolting," Fiona replied.

Paul looked somewhat superciliously at her.

"Are you really going to keep up this pose of virginity?" he said. "It's amusing for a little while, but you really can't do the baby eyes stunt indefinitely.

"And anyhow," he added in a kinder tone, "I should be careful not to offend his Lordship. He's an old devil

19

for complaining, and he's one of the best customers here."

Fiona nodded her head.

"I gathered that, from the fuss that's been made over him."

"Don't you forget it," Paul advised. "Oh, Lord—the band's going to play a tango. That means we've got to start this dance."

He and Fiona got up and began to dance.

Two or three other couples gradually drifted on to the dance floor, but there were very few of them, and Fiona was all the time conscious that Lord Winthrop's eyes were following every movement she made.

They went through all the swaying movements and intricate cross-steps of an exhibition tango, but all the time she was wondering how she could avoid the man who was watching her across the room.

She had a vague presentiment of nastiness, a desire to avoid him at any cost.

She knew Clare would think her a fool, and Paul would give her no sympathy. There was no one else to whom she could confide her fears.

After all, they might be unfounded, yet at the same time she felt he was going to be objectionable.

She had been so comfortable these last weeks at Paglioni's. The late hours had been difficult at first, but now she had got used to them and had learnt to sleep, in spite of the noise in the mews, until nearly luncheon time.

She had certainly not managed to save any money, in fact she had already expended next week's pay on a new dress, which she had been obliged to buy.

She could not face the thought of finding another job, and at the same time she realised that the one she held depended entirely on herself.

One complaint might be sufficient to bring that curt dismissal, and put her back again into those long queues.

"How morbid I'm getting," she thought, giving herself mentally a little shake, "and how stupid, just because one old man asks me to supper!"

She looked quickly round at him. He was watching her still. As she got back to her table, she said to Paul, with a sudden gust of anger,

"How I hate this life!"

He looked at her in surprise.

"If you know a better job . . ."

Half-ashamed of herself, Fiona laughed up at him.

"I don't," she confessed.

"I've met worse myself," Paul answered; taking a long drink of water.

Rising to his feet, he walked across the room to ask a gay dowager of sixty-five for the next fox-trot. As he passed a mirror, he gave himself a self-satisfied glance.

"He's too stupid to want anything better," Fiona told herself.

Then she saw that Lord Winthrop had risen, and was making his way towards her.

CHAPTER TWO

There was one man who came to the restaurant whom Fiona admired very much.

She did not know who he was for some time, but at last she discovered that his name was Jim Macdonald, the son of an elderly peer who owned vast estates in Scotland.

It was Clare who found his photograph in the *Tatler*, and showed it to Fiona, and the very next night—for coincidences of that kind do happen—he came across to their table and asked her to dance.

He was with another man, both of them in dinner-jackets, and when they had come into Paglioni's, obviously after the theatre, Fiona, on seeing him, had hoped that he would come and ask her for a dance.

Always when she had seen him before he had been accompanied by women, and she had especially noticed that he was never with the noisy young things to whom she had taken such a dislike.

He was generally with the young married set, and with the most beautiful of them.

They were seldom a big party—four, or perhaps six —and they always seemed to be interested intensely in what they were talking about.

In fact, they danced usually very little, perhaps only two or three times during the evening.

Jim Macdonald was very tall and very distinguished-looking. Even among such a crowd of diverse types as was to be seen, night after night, at Paglioni's, he stood out.

He was fair, with grey eyes which always had a twinkle in them, and while not good-looking in any stereotyped way, he gave the impression of very English, out-door handsomeness.

He did not ask for an introduction to Fiona in the ordinary way, but walked up to their table, and said,

"Will you dance with me, please?"

She accepted immediately, thankful that she was free. They danced round for a moment or two in silence, and then Jim spoke first.

"I felt you must be a very good dancer," he said. "I was quite right."

He had a deep and charming voice, and Fiona smiled happily in response.

"I am glad you are not disappointed," she answered.

"I'm not," he said. "I love dancing with anybody who's good, but I am afraid I am not much use myself —I don't get enough practice."

"But I think you're very good," she answered and added, "I'm not just saying that."

"Thank you," he said, and after that conversation seemed easy between them.

Fiona went back to his table and had supper with him, and she was surprised to find how much they had in common to talk about.

It was strange, because their lives had both been so different, yet somehow there was a lot to say, a lot to discuss, and it was with surprise that Fiona suddenly realised that the room was nearly empty, and that the evening was over.

"Look here," Jim said, "we must meet again. Come and lunch with me to-morrow."

Eagerly Fiona accepted, far too pleased to hesitate.

They lunched quietly in a small restaurant in Dover Street, and over an excellent meal they talked and talked of everything. Jim had done such a lot in his life.

He had been brought up in Scotland, on the family

estates; he had been old enough to serve in the last year of the war, and after that was over he had found himself unable to settle down to country life.

So he had gone out to Africa, where he had a farm for nearly a year, returning only because his father was ill and growing too old to manage his estates himself.

Once back in England, he had found it impossible to get away again, though he had travelled for short spaces of time all over the world.

He had hated to have no occupation, and had taken up the technical side of motoring, being now a director of one of the biggest combines in the country.

And yet, with all this experience, he was so young, so eager to sample everything in life, and finding it all amusing.

He was spoilt to a certain extent, for he was too fascinating for women to leave him alone.

He had been run after and fêted until he almost believed that femininity was merely an extra entertainment put into the world for his amusement.

He did not compliment Fiona as the other men she had met at Paglioni's had done, nor did he attempt in any way to flirt with her.

But she was women enough to know that she attracted him, and to know quite surely that they would often meet again.

While she was dressing in her little mews bedroom to go out that night, she thought again and again of Jim, and of his charm, and it was only when she was nearly dressed that she realised with a sickening remembrance that she was having supper with Lord Winthrop.

Her first supper with him had been quite uneventful, yet she could not rid herself of the feeling that he was unpleasantly dangerous to her.

The first night they had supper together he had talked quite interestingly, but he would try to press her knee under the table, and to hold her hand.

Then he had offered to take her home, but she had been clever enough to dissuade him. She had promised

24

to give another girl a lift, she said—she had no idea he would be kind enough to offer.

"Next time you must let me take you," he said, and she had to agree.

He asked her a great many questions about herself, but she managed to make her answers as evasive as possible. She had no desire to discuss her life, her inclinations or her desires with this old *roué*.

She had heard quite a lot about him by this time from Clare. He had a lot of money, derived originally by his grandfather from beer.

He had no son, but two daughters, who were married, and a wife who preferred to spend most of her time in Paris, having "affairs" with men who were young enough to be her own sons.

Lord Winthrop was a lonely man, but he was never for long without a mistress of one sort or another. He ran very true to type and did not care for anyone who was not a blonde.

"I'm quite safe from him," said Clare, "which is unfortunate, for I wouldn't mind going with the old boy for a bit. One of the girls here got over a hundred pounds in cash from him, and a marvellous fur coat."

"I don't want either," Fiona said, and shivered, but Clare laughed at her.

"Don't be a silly," she said, "you've got to take the plunge sooner or later, and you might just as well do it with somebody rich."

"Perhaps he won't really like me in that sort of way," Fiona answered.

But Clare laughed incredulously, and she knew her hope was quite without foundation.

"I dare say I can stave him off," she thought, "if only I can think of enough excuses not to go home with him."

She thought wildly of inventing a devoted mother, but knew that he would not believe her.

To-day she had been so happy with Jim that she had quite forgotten this Damoclesian sword hanging over her head to-night, but now, as she was dressing, it returned to her with terrifying clearness.

She could not afford to put on an unbecoming dress, or try and make herself look plain—she knew that Paglioni's eagle eye would be on her.

The other night, she had been told off for not drinking champagne when offered it. She had been feeling tired and headachy, and champagne was inclined to make her head worse.

She had sat at some old man's table, and he had offered her champagne, but she had refused, preferring a brandy-and-soda, so he had ordered only a half-bottle of champagne instead of a bottle, and Paglioni had seen.

The next day he had called Fiona into his office.

"Whatever a client drinks, you drink, and you understand that with a client, if possible, your drink is to be champagne. I shall not speak again."

Fiona understood that threat in his words, and escaped, thankful that she had received nothing worse than a talking to.

It was raining when she got downstairs.

The one thing she dreaded was rain, for it spoilt the wave in her hair, and meant there was every likelihood of her arriving at Paglioni's with a creased and mud-spattered dress.

Luckily she was able to get on a 'bus without waiting too long.

She had her evening shoes in a parcel, but as she fumbled with her bag she dropped it and the shoes fell with a little clatter on the floor of the bus.

A man sitting opposite picked them up and handed them back to her.

"Thank you," she said.

He was a young man, about twenty-eight or twenty-nine, well dressed in a cheapish way, and with quite a nice smile.

To her dismay, she found she had only ten shillings in her purse. She had forgotten to get change. The conductor looked at it disapprovingly.

"Please let me," came a voice from opposite, and twopence was tendered.

"But I couldn't let you . . . I mean, have you got change for ten shillings?" Fiona said.

The stranger crossed and sat down beside her.

"I'm afraid I haven't," he explained quietly.

The conductor, having taken the money and clipped the ticket, had already disappeared, glad that he was not obliged to try and produce change.

"It's terribly kind of you, but what shall I do about it?" Fiona asked.

"Nothing," he said. "You can't very well waste a penny-halfpenny stamp sending it back to me."

They both laughed.

"I've often seen you on this bus," he said.

"Yes, I generally catch one about this time," Fiona answered.

"Are you going to work?" he asked. "I am."

"Yes," Fiona replied. "I work at Paglioni's."

"I'm going to Fleet Street—I'm on the night shift of the *Daily Mercury*."

"How interesting," Fiona said. "Do you like it?"

"Quite," he replied. "I've been at it some time. I don't know that there's much future in the smaller jobs on a newspaper, but, still, it's better than nothing."

"That's what I feel," Fiona said, and then the thought of the evening came over her, and she added, "sometimes I doubt it, though."

"It's worse for a woman than a man," her new friend said. "It always seems wrong to me for a woman to be working."

"How old-fashioned!" Fiona murmured.

"Yes, isn't it?" he replied. "But I always feel if I ever married I should hate my wife to work."

"She might have to, unless you're an editor by that time," Fiona said.

"Not a chance!" he replied. "Oh—this is where you get out. May we meet again some time? My name is Donald Burn."

"I'd love to—and thank you again for the twopence,"

Fiona replied, and waving to him she jumped off the bus, and hurried away into the darkness.

"What a nice man," she thought, as she went along the greasy street, holding her dress high above her ankles.

As she neared Paglioni's, a large Rolls-Royce passed her and drew up at the door, and when she turned into the waiters' entrance at the side, she saw step out Lord Winthrop, wearing a fur-collared overcoat.

"My Lord arrives!" thought Fiona.

She swung open the door, and, hurrying past the steaming kitchens, ran up the back stairs to the ladies' cloakroom.

*   *   *

"He's a horrible old man!" Fiona said.

She was having tea with Donald Burn at a small tea-shop in Chelsea.

This was the third time they had met, and they were great friends.

She found his outlook on the world, although tinged with journalese, interesting and vital. He had already taught her to be more observant, to find a story in the dullest building or the most dowdy person.

Incidentally he had managed to get her employed as a free-lance gossip writer for the women's column of his paper.

She received five shillings for every paragraph accepted, and as she had plenty of chance of observing society doings, there was a likelihood of her being able to add to her earnings every week.

Quite inexperienced in how to write gossip, she naturally had to submit what she wrote to Donald first, and he had shown her how easily news could be manufactured out of the most slender information.

Proudly to-day she had shown him her first cheque for ten shillings, for "two paragraphs supplied and used" by "Lady Maud," who wrote the "Doings about Town" in the *Daily Mercury*.

It was while Donald was pulling together her paragraphs for the following day that he mentioned Lord Winthrop.

"He's generally good for a paragraph," he said.

"He's a horrible old man," Fiona repeated. "Thank goodness he's gone away for the week to Scotland."

"Splendid!" Donald cried. "Why didn't you tell me before?" And he wrote hastily—

"Lord Winthrop has left London for a few days for his estates in Scotland. A well-known angler and a great sportsman, he will be eagerly welcomed in the Highlands, although missed by his many acquaintances in London.

"Lord Winthrop's house in Park Lane is full of treasures, the famous Winthrop diamond being one of them. It is a long time since the public has had a chance of seeing it, but people are hoping that Lady Winthrop will wear it at the Court Ball in a month's time, for which she will undoubtedly return from Paris, where she is at present."

While he was writing, Fiona was thinking of her last encounter with the subject of Donald's paragraph.

She could still feel his horrible soft, licentious kisses on her mouth, could still feel herself striving not to protest wildly, not to cry out, and even strike at this man who was insulting her with his caresses.

When the Rolls had finally stopped at her address, she had sprung out and rushed into the house, hardly able to murmur good-bye.

She hated him with such violence that she felt, were it to happen again, she would be unable to contain herself, and she was filled with horror at the knowledge that on his return it would happen again.

He was not satisfied, he had not finished with her yet, and she knew she could not refuse to see him, or restrain his ardours, without losing her job.

Paglioni himself had bowed them into the Rolls-Royce that night, as they left the restaurant.

His smirking pleasantries were all for Lord Winthrop, yet at the same time she detected approval in his voice, as he said, "Good night, Miss Mayne."

Were she to offend Lord Winthrop, she knew that her position would not last one day. She would go, and someone else blonde and pretty would take her place.

However, he was away, and she was thrilled with a new idea of having a tiny flat of her own.

Donald had found her one, and though the rent was fifteen shillings a week, she could just manage it, if she could continue to make a little extra money on the *Daily Mercury*.

The two rooms were very small, but she would have a home of her own, and in a vicinity not quite so noisy and sordid as that in which she was living at present.

The flat was over a shop, on the top floor up a number of stairs, the floors below being used for the shop itself and for storage.

The man who owned the shop was a friend of Donald's, and had intended asking a higher rent, but Donald had persuaded him to accept fifteen shillings.

Fiona, having seen the rooms, was enthusiastic as to their possibilities.

The trouble was furniture, and Donald's idea was that she should wait before moving in, and collect a few pieces each week. But for once her enthusiasm carried her away, and drawing ten pounds of her precious capital from the bank, she spent it on furnishing.

Even then the rooms were bare, but they promised themselves many trips, in search of bargains, to the Caledonian Market and Petticoat Lane on a Sunday.

Fiona was aware that Donald was falling in love with her, but though she liked him very much indeed, she realised—although she would hardly confess it, even to herself—that she was already in love with someone else.

She had seen Jim Macdonald twice since their luncheon together. One night he had supper at Paglioni's, and another time he had taken her for a drive in his car.

She had loved the drive, although they had not gone far, only out to Richmond Park, where they had tea at a hotel and then back to London.

It was getting dark as they turned homewards, and Jim tucked a rug warmly round her. Then, as they drove off, he put his hand on hers.

"Warm?" he said.

And Fiona had answered, "So happy!"

Jim had turned his eyes from the road for a second and looked at her face raised to his, dim in the twilight and the reflection from the dashboard.

"Dear little Fiona!" he said, "you are so sweet."

His fingers closed on hers, and he had driven home precariously with one hand, and Fiona was in a heaven of happiness.

To-night she might see him again, and to-morrow she would move into her new flat. She thought of telling Jim about it, and could not help hoping that one day perhaps he would come and see her there.

She thought of Jim all the time. At night she went to sleep with his name on her lips, and slept only to dream of him. The first thing she visualised when she awoke was his face as he had last smiled at her.

She had squeezed Clare dry of all the information that she had about him.

She had begged her to find more, to think of more, to remember where she had seen him written about, in what paper and when. Clare had done her best to oblige, but even her information was limited, and at time inaccurate.

She could not remember with whom Jim had been having an "affair" last season—had it been Lady Trence or Lady Maxwell? She could not remember.

"They are both such great friends, you see," she said. "They always seemed to come here together with your Jim. I don't know which it was. Sometimes I thought it was one, and sometimes the other—anyway, I wasn't taking all that interest in him myself."

To Fiona Jim never talked of other women. He had never mentioned any of them.

Unlike most of the men, when he came to Paglioni's with his friends he bowed to Fiona and smiled at her, though he did not come across and speak to her.

"Who's that?" Fiona heard a partner of his ask him, as they danced past her table, and he smiled at her.

The girl he was dancing with was pretty, but spoilt by a rather sulky expression. She was young, but evidently *blasé* already.

Fiona did not hear Jim's reply, but noticed the girl looked at her several times with a lazy interest.

She had never felt so alive, as she did after the dull, apathetic time she had spent with her father, and the awful loneliness after the funeral when his things were being straightened out.

It was such a change, this different world, a world bounded by restrictions, but nevertheless bringing people and interest into her life.

Donald finished her paragraphs and put them in his pocket.

"I'll give them to the editor myself," he said.

Fiona thanked him, and he paid the bill. Outside twilight was just falling. The King's Road was a blaze of yellow lights, flaring over the vegetable shops which were thronged with shoppers, or shining dimly in windows set with antique furniture.

The trees of Royal Avenue were showing the first signs of approaching spring, and fat pigeons were already roosting in their branches.

"This is where my home will be to-morrow," Fiona thought, looking about her.

It seemed homely and cosy, somehow, as if the people were bent on domestic duties, not concerned with the grandeur of Mayfair or the bustle of Oxford Street, as were those where she lived now.

And Donald would be there, only two streets away. She smiled at him, in the light of a pawnbroker's window, and slipped her arm through his.

"You are kind to me, Donald," she said.

32

"You know I want you to be happy," he replied, very seriously.

"There's our 'bus," said Fiona quickly, suddenly glad of an excuse to escape. "Hurry, or we shan't catch it," They ran across the road and jumped aboard.

Twenty minutes later Fiona was alone in her little room. Putting out the light, she lay down on the bed and closed her eyes. She was tired, and yet she must be fresh and gay for to-night.

She wondered if she would see Jim; she had a feeling she might.

"Jim, Jim!" she whispered his name aloud.

How terribly he attracted her! She could quite understand all the women running after him. She was running herself, and didn't care who knew it.

"Jim!" she whispered again.

* * *

"I love you, Jim," Fiona whispered brokenly, and in answer Jim kissed her again.

They had spent a wonderful evening, dancing at Paglioni's. Jim had come in there just after eleven o'clock.

He had invited Fiona to his table, and she had gone across to him with a heart throbbing with excitement.

They had danced together and it was to Fiona as though some vital spark in her had been communicated to Jim, and that he looked at her in a different way from what he had before.

"Let's go," he said at last, "I'll make it all right with Paglioni."

His car was waiting, and Fiona felt the cool wind on her hot face as they sped through the deserted streets. He drew up the car outside the huge Mayfair building, and in silence they climbed the wide stairs to his flat door.

A log fire burned in an open grate, and Jim turned on the discreetly-shaded lamps while Fiona sank on to a low sofa.

33

She sat looking at him, then he turned and her eyes met his. As if in answer to some command, she rose to her feet and walked into his outstretched arms.

"Darling—darling!" he murmured, as his lips met hers.

It seemed to her hours before she lifted her face to his and said, "I do . . . love you so."

"Don't Fiona—don't," Jim commanded.

He suddenly let her go, his arms falling to his sides, and then as he saw the bewildered look on her face, he held her again almost roughly.

"Fiona, Fiona!" he murmured, "you go to my head!"

He kissed her again and again. She was panting a little, and breathless from his kissing and from excitement when he let her go.

Fiona steadied herself against a chair, and then sat down. Jim stood for a moment, gazing into space pensively, as if searching the future.

Then he put his hand under her chin and lifted up her face.

"Do you really love me, Fiona?" he asked.

There was no need for an answer, he saw it trembling on her mouth and in the sincerity of her eyes raised to him.

There was no need for her to whisper a word to him, and he watched her bury her face against his arms.

"Oh, my darling," Jim cried, then his voice changed, "and I love you. I knew it, Fiona—I knew it the first moment I saw you. Listen, my dear. I have been fighting against this. I have been trying not to come and see you, trying not to let you down.

"I have been trying to think of you as one of the millions of girls I meet every day of my life. But it's something deeper than that.

"I knew it the moment I saw you, and I know it, and —it is something which I can't control—something I've never felt before."

He walked away from her, then he spun round suddenly.

"It is love, Fiona, love for the first time in my life."

34

Fiona sat with shining eyes, her hands clenched tightly. He loved her—he loved her, that was all she could think of.

Her brain was reeling, and then, before the real wonder of it could penetrate, he was beside her, putting his arms around her, his face on a level with hers.

"Why didn't I go away, Fiona? Tell me that. I realised the danger as soon as I saw you, as soon as we danced together, and I saw your darling little face within reach of mine.

"You'll never know, Fiona, how much I wanted to kiss you the very first time we danced together. I knew it was madness. I knew the only chance was for me to go abroad, but I didn't, darling, because I'm weak and I'm a fool, and now we both are in this terrible mess."

"What mess?" Fiona asked.

Suddenly her happiness ebbed away from her, leaving fear like an icy hand clutching at her heart. For a moment, Jim dropped his head against her knees.

"I'm a cad, Fiona dear. You ought to have known that the first time you saw me. I'm a cad."

"Why, Jim—why? Tell me. Oh, my dear, tell me why."

Fiona, emboldened by his misery, touched him gently with her hand.

"Listen, Fiona," he said, "I'll tell you. Last year I was hunting in Leicestershire, and I had a rather dangerous fall. I was carried to the nearest house, which happened to be the home of the local Squire.

"He was an outwardly bluff, good-humoured man, but he didn't seem very glad to see me, which of course wasn't surprising, especially as I had to have a couple of doctors.

"However, he gave me the best room in the house, although for the first few days I was far too ill to care where I was. It was about the fourth day of my convalescence that I first saw my hostess.

"She came unexpectedly into my room, and she took me completely by surprise. I found myself apologising

35

to her, and listening to her assurances that I was no trouble. But she . . .

"I wish I could describe her to you, Fiona, because it is very difficult, and yet so important for you to understand what I am trying to tell you. She is not very tall, very small-boned, and I suppose most people would call her thin.

"Yet her body seemed unimportant—it is her face at which everyone looks as soon as they meet her. A white face, not classically beautiful, but surmounted by deep red hair the colour of cherry-wood.

"Her eyes are very large and grey, they seem to be looking far away to horizons that other people cannot see. That all sounds unusual and not exactly attractive, and yet her mouth is the key to her personality.

"It is always smiling a little, yet wistfully, as if she were frightened of the impulse. It is a beautiful, generous, almost passionate mouth, yet even when she is laughing there is a touch of fear in its movement.

"Oh, Fiona—it is very hard to tell you this, but I must. I want to make you understand. I said that Ann seemed fearful when she laughed. I'll tell you the reason.

"Her husband was damnably cruel to her . . . not in the way of a navvy, who comes home Saturday nights and beats his wife, but in a far more subtle way, in which it is impossible for a woman to obtain relief or help.

"It was mental cruelty, but not even of the usual type of mental cruelty, which works itself out by being rude, disagreeable or unkind in front of people. It was of an even more subtle order.

"Ann's husband—and I'm speaking the truth, Fiona —Ann's husband treated his wife as if she were mad.

"He never said anything to her, but everything she did he treated with kindly tolerance, as though he were a doctor humouring an unnerved patient.

"It took me a long time to tumble to this. I didn't guess it at once. At first I saw a man very sweet and gentle with his young and attractive wife.

"And then, intrigued perhaps by her air of wistfulness, her rather hesitating manner of expressing an opinion even to him, I began to realise that something was very wrong, that there was an undercurrent beneath this surface of pleasantry which I couldn't understand.

"I was there several weeks. The doctors refused to allow me to be moved, and when I was in the convalescent stage it became a habit for them to use my bedroom as a sitting-room, so that I should have companionship.

"I think the doctor must have said that it would be good for me to be able to talk and take an interest in other things besides my own helpless body.

"Anyway, they were continually with me, together or separately, and it was not until nearly the end of my stay that I really realised that I was watching a diabolic form of torture.

"By this time, I had grown very fond of Ann—no, I'll tell you the truth, Fiona, I fancied myself in love with her.

"Imagine a sick man with nothing else to interest him, with no other people to see but these two, one rather uninteresting man, the other an extremely attractive woman. You won't be surprised that I fell in love with her.

"Fell in love only in my imagination, but at the time it seemed very real;—and Ann fell in love with me.

"It was when we had finally confessed to each other our affection that she told me the story of her marriage and what she was suffering.

"She had been an only child of adoring parents. She was extremely intelligent and would have taken all sorts of degrees and honours had she been at a University.

"Her father was a professor and he had brought up his daughter with a man's education of all classical subjects. She was very well-read and tremendously interested in life.

"Suddenly her home was shattered by the death of both her parents in an accident—a motor accident, I think it was, and while she was alone, bewildered and

37

utterly miserable, she met the man who was later to become her husband.

"He was older than she was, and very kind. She was so shaken and lonely that she turned to the first kind arms that were held out to her. It was only after they were married she realised how little they had in common.

"Her husband had spent all his life in the country. He had never read a book. He was interested in his animals and his sports and was to outward appearance an ordinary country gentleman.

"But he cherished an extraordinary inferiority complex which made him dislike any form of intellectual superiority. He himself was only concerned with and attracted by Ann's looks.

"He saw a miserable, helpless, but very beautiful girl, and he required nothing else besides. He was the sort of man who liked to be superior, the type that considered woman a fragile creature and likes her to be dependent on man's strength for all her needs.

"When she recovered from the unhappiness of her parents' loss, and showed the first signs of intelligent thought and criticism of things around her, he was definitely alarmed.

"At first he bullied her a little, laughing and sneering at all her interest, especially her love of reading.

"Then as her personality gradually became real to him, and he found that Ann was his superior in every intellectual way, his persecution of her mind took a more definite and dangerous form.

"He refused to invite or listen to her opinions on any subject. If she expressed one, he said,

" 'There, there, dear,' good-humouredly, as though he were speaking to a child who was reciting some extravagant fancy.

"Physically, she still attracted him, after five years of marriage, as she had when he first married her; perhaps because of this very intellectual quality he so disliked.

"It took Ann three years to discover that she was up

against a brick wall of fanatical obstinacy and stupidity. Then she capitulated.

"I never heard her express an opinion or join voluntarily in a conversation when her husband was present.

"Alone with me, after she forgot her shyness, she chattered away, begging me to argue with her as though to her controversy was like water to a man dying of thirst.

"At first she even seemed to enjoy my conversation more than my kisses, but, Fiona—this is hard to say to you—you can understand later how much my kisses meant to her, for she had really loathed her husband for over two years.

"She was terrified of him in a sort of hypnotised, hysterical way—stupid it would seem to us, who live free lives untrammelled by others, but she was utterly dependent on him.

"She saw very few people, she did not hunt herself, and the neighbours who were around were either hard hunting people who lived for nothing else, or society which came down from London for just a few days in the week.

"He did not encourage her to see people. He liked a woman to be in her place in the house dependent only on him, requiring no other society or interests save him and his.

"At first he was entirely unsuspicious of me and tolerant of my existence in their solitary household, for the simple reason that he had a healthy man's contempt for anyone who was laid up.

"He had never known a day's illness in his life, and he treated anyone who was ill with the same contemptuous superiority as he treated his wife.

"His attitude towards everything in life was that of a bully confident of his physical strength. At last, to cut a long story short, I begged Ann to run away with me.

"She was beset with tremors and fright, she could hardly believe it was possible for her to escape from her prison and her gaoler. For a long time she would not decide, then finally I had to leave.

"I was quite well enough to move, the doctors said, and further treatment could be continued in London. I left, and a week after I had gone, Ann ran away from her husband. But she did not run to me.

"She is an extraordinarily straightforward person, Fiona, and she thought that her being divorced might prejudice me socially and in business. Instead, she merely left her husband and refused to return to him.

"There was no mention of my name in the matter, and though he was suspicious he could not in any way justify his suspicions.

"That was a year ago, but it is only a few weeks ago that I heard that Ann's husband is giving her a divorce. Ann was clever enough to know that he was the type of man who could not live without a woman.

"He has already found one whom he wishes to marry and Ann is divorcing him as quickly as possible. She is wholeheartedly mine, but in the meantime I have found you.

"This makes me seem a heartless beast, Fiona, but I can't help it. I have only seen Ann twice in a year."

There was nothing to say. Fiona sat dumb with the misery of it all. Jim was looking away from her across the room.

The firelight was on his clear-cut features, on his hair which waved away from his broad forehead, and on his serious mouth.

His story had swept away her happiness.

They sat for a long time silent, then Fiona turned to him with a broken sob, and held out her hands. He took them, stood up and drew her gently to her feet.

"You'd better go, Fiona darling," he said. "There's not much more to be said between us. I'll try to avoid seeing you. There's nothing else I can do, is there?"

"Oh, Jim!" Fiona cried.

The misery of it hurt her more than she could have believed possible. She swayed against him so that he put out his arm to support her, and in another moment she was lying in his arms.

"Fiona, my darling," he murmured, his mouth against her hair. She lifted her arms and put them round his neck.

"I shall never, never forget you, Jim. I shall love you always, I think," she said.

He kissed her mouth, and they were suddenly strained together. His kisses grew more and more violent, till she seemed to be drifting into a dream of wonderful feeling. She seemed to have no will of her own.

She could only stay there in an absolute ecstasy of happiness, feeling his hot fierce kisses on her mouth, feeling his arms strong like steel around her, knowing a thrill which she had never experienced before.

Then suddenly Jim turned away from her, turned and walked to the mantelpiece and stood with his back to the room, his hands over his eyes.

"Go, Fiona, for God's sake, go," he said, in a voice quite unlike his own. "I love you, darling, I want you. This is absolute hell."

Fiona picked up her coat and put it on with shaking fingers, then she stood waiting a little timorously for him. He faced her.

"If I can't offer you marriage, Fiona, I'm not prepared to offer you anything else, though heaven knows I'd give anything in the world to make love to you."

He took her white hand showing beneath the shabby cuff of her old black coat, and kissed it very gently.

"Bless you, my darling," he said. "I shall never, never forget how wonderful you have been to me."

Without a word they walked slowly down the dark stairs of the flats. Outside a solitary taxi was ambling its way down the street. Jim hired it, and put Fiona inside.

"I'm not coming with you. I must say good-bye now," he said.

Again he kissed her hand, and then he directed the taximan to her flat and paid him.

Her last glimpse of Jim was as he stood watching the

taxi till it was out of sight, immobile in a deserted square.

At home in her flat, Fiona paced the floor of her sitting-room all night. She could not sleep. She undressed and lay down on her bed, but it was useless.

She could still feel Jim's kisses on her mouth, his arms around her, the thrill of him coursing through her veins.

Once for a moment she dozed to imagine he was with her in reality, to awake only to find the loneliness of reality insupportable.

She made herself a cup of hot cocoa on her tiny stove and tried to read, but the words in the book meant absolutely nothing to her throbbing brain. She could not keep still.

She moved slowly up and down the room until at last, through her small window, she saw the dawn break over the roofs of Chelsea, and then her control gave way and she broke into a passion of tears.

She cried for a long while, then utterly worn-out sank into a dreamless slumber.

She was awakened by a heavy tap on her door, and she opened it to find a messenger boy with a huge box of flowers.

They were from Jim—her heart told her that, although there was no card in them.

Masses of white flowers and red. They lay in their long, narrow box, "like a coffin," Fiona thought for a moment miserably, "a coffin of their love."

For a long time she could not undo the wrapping further, but sat on her heels staring at the box as it lay in front of her, full of its fragrant blossoms.

It was nearly one o'clock before she finally roused herself to wash and dress.

She had remembered vaguely through her misery that she was lunching with Donald.

She was hardly ready—for it took some time to hide the ravages of her tears—when he arrived.

He waited in the little sitting-room, but if he noticed the flowers that were arranged in profusion all over the tiny room, put in old jam-jars and tins for lack of vases, he said nothing.

Only when she came out, pale and drawn, her eyes swollen and dark-rimmed, did he take a quick glance at her face, and ask, "Are you ill, Fiona?"

She shook her head, and without another word they went slowly down the narrow stairs into the street.

Fiona walked along, too dazed and dizzy to care where they were going.

Presently she found herself in one of those small shops which cater mostly for vegetarians.

As she walked, her whole being had been racked with memories of Jim. She could hear nothing but his voice, and see nothing but his eyes, and when she stopped she felt his arms around her.

"Jim, Jim, Jim," her footsteps seemed to ring on the pavement, and when they crossed the road it was only Donald's hand on her arm that held her back from being run down by the approaching traffic.

"What will you have to eat?" she heard Donald say.

It suddenly struck her that these were the first words he had spoken since he had asked her if she were ill before they had left her flat.

She hoped that he would not be inquisitive, and then, rousing herself to pay attention to him, noticed that he himself was looking extremely unwell.

There was a worried look about him that she never seemed to have noticed before.

He was studying the menu, but there was obviously an effort of concentration about him, as though he did not care but was forcing himself to show some interest in their order.

Finally, he chose fish pie, and Fiona, glad to be saved from a choice of dishes, none of which she wanted either, agreed to have the same.

When the waitress went away there was an awkward silence between them; awkward, because though they had not spoken before they had been unconscious of their lack of words.

43

Yet now they were both thinking rapidly of some subject on which to start a conversation.

At last Fiona said, "What's the matter with you, Donald?" hoping that it was not anything to do with her that was causing this haggardness and general air of anxiety.

She knew that Donald had been in love with her for some time, yet she felt at this moment she could not bear the declaration which had been trembling on his lips for weeks past.

When Donald raised his eyes at last to hers, she saw that her fears of a proposal at this moment in this dreadful smelling restaurant, were quite unfounded.

"Fiona," he said hoarsely, "I've got a terrible thing to ask you, so awful, I am shocked and ashamed at having to do it. You are my last hope, the only person I can turn to."

"Why, what's the matter, Donald?" Fiona was startled for a moment out of herself by the desperation in his tone. She leaned forward eagerly, forgetting her own troubles.

"I have got to find a hundred pounds," Donald said abruptly.

"Good heavens, why?" Fiona ejaculated.

Donald pushed his plate further away from him, put his elbows on the table.

"I'll try and explain, Fiona dear. For God's sake forgive me for asking you to do it. It's my younger brother. You have never met him, for the simple reason that he doesn't lodge with me in town, but lives with my mother.

"He goes down every night, and though we are very fond of each other, he is too many years my junior for us to be great friends. He's got quite a good post as cashier in a tea merchant's in the City.

"He has been there for some two years now, and we imagined has been very happy. I saw him last night. He is a fair-haired, cheerful-looking youth as a rule, but last night he was all shot to pieces.

"He was utterly miserable, and drank far too much. Finally I got the story out of him.

"He had been gambling heavily, gambling because he wanted to keep up the rather rich effect of the other men whom he considers his friends.

"You can imagine what has happened. He has taken money from his firm, trusting to put it back before accounts-day by bringing off a big coup on the race-course. Does one ever pick a winner under those circumstances?

"It is hardly likely, is it? He started with ten pounds —ten pounds is a lot of money for someone in his position to find. He plunged into debt to between fifteen and twenty-five.

"He says that he then went mad, and gambled wildly and unreasonably in an effort to reinstate himself. Last night he knew that he had only forty-eight hours in which to find the money and return it, unless his theft was to be discovered.

"It means prison, Fiona, if he is discovered, and his absolute ruination. He's a nice boy, but he's a weak character, and if he once found himself without a job he would go to the devil for good.

"He is only twenty-two, and I have got to save him. That's why I have come to you, Fiona. It's awful of me to ask you, and I know that I have no right to, but what else can I do?

"Who else can I appeal to? I have no well-off friends, and even if I had, a hundred pounds is a lot to ask. Will you lend me yours, Fiona? Will you?

"I swear I'll return it some way or another. If I had the time, I wouldn't ask you for it, but I cannot raise a hundred pounds in two days."

"Poor Donald!"

Fiona was genuinely upset by his story, and saw how terribly the telling of it had hurt him.

She understood a little of the agony Donald must have experienced last night, the fight he must have had with himself before he would make up his mind to ask her for money.

She leaned across the table and touched his hand.

45

"You did absolutely right to come to me, Donald. Of course you can have my money. But it's only ninety pounds. Can you find the other ten?"

She saw the change to relief in his face, and he gripped her hand until it hurt.

"Oh, Fiona," he murmured.

For one awful moment she thought he was going to break down, but she talked quickly to give him time to get himself under control.

"It's on deposit, Donald," she said. "I'm afraid I can't draw it out right away, but if we went straight up to the bank now, the bank manager would arrange for you to be able to have it to-morrow night. Let's go, I hate this place."

They paid for their lunch which they left untouched, and walked out into the street. They jumped on a 'bus and went to Fiona's bank, which was on the north side of the Park.

"Fiona, I can't thank you," Donald said as they came out of the bank. "It's no use my trying to explain to you, but I think you know that you have done a marvellous thing to save the boy's life."

"That's all right, Donald," Fiona said, putting her arm through his. "Don't try to thank me. You pay it back when you can."

She gave a little laugh, trying to relieve the tension of their conversation. They walked towards the Underground station.

"Would you mind very much if I went down to the City," asked Donald, "and told my brother? I hate to leave you, Fiona, but the boy ought to hear."

"Of course," said Fiona. "Tell him that I really am happy I have been able to help."

"God bless you, Fiona!" Donald said.

Fiona started to walk back through the Park. It was a lovely afternoon.

Alone, she found her thoughts returning to Jim. She knew how she had looked forward in the evening to catching a glimpse of him at Paglioni's.

Whilst she was by no means happy, she was not so

46

intensely miserable, with that dazed feeling that she had experienced when she first realised that the day had come with no hope of seeing Jim again.

She had watched the door in the hope of seeing him, tall, good-looking, come into the rose-lighted restaurant.

She had dressed and tried to look attractive for one reason only. She had turned to new clothes, new ways of hair-dressing, merely that she should look lovely enough to be worthy of his notice.

Fiona sat down on a bench, and as she did so she felt a run draw in her stocking.

"My last pair!" she murmured ruefully. "I wonder when I am going to get any more."

Then is struck her for the first time that she was without any backing whatsoever, now that she had given away her tiny capital to Donald.

Always before it had been a bulwark between her and the fear of starvation.

She had always felt that after all one could live for a long time on a hundred pounds.

Although she had vowed to herself that she would not break into it except in dire emergency, it was a comforting, warm feeling to know that the money was there, in the safe custody of the bank.

She shrugged her shoulders.

"One thing is I needn't wear stockings at night. Luckily they won't show under the long dresses."

Then the idea of a new dress started to trouble her, for she knew every possible change had been wrought on her red to make it seem different.

Sitting on the park bench she opened her purse, and looked at the ten-shilling note inside.

She had paid her rent for the week, and that was all that was left, to pay her fares and her shilling-in-the-slot gas-meter, and her food for the rest of the week—unless she were lucky enough to get a tip.

"How is it possible to get a new dress out of that?" she thought. "It isn't!"

At the same time, a little cold fear crept into her. Supposing Paglioni was annoyed? Supposing she lost her job? She had nothing to save her now. Her money was gone—in a week she would be starving.

"I've got to do something about it," she said. "I shall have to."

For a moment she caught herself wishing that she had kept just five pounds back of her capital from Donald, then despised herself for the thought.

She knew that Donald would find difficulty enough in finding ten pounds by to-morrow.

He lived in lodgings, and he could have few assets of his own bar his clothes.

While she was dressing the tears would come to her eyes, and she realised, apart from her misery about Jim and her anxiety about her clothes, she was desperately hungry.

She had eaten no lunch and her head was aching, but she knew that would pass off as soon as she had had some supper.

She put on the red chiffon, and recognised with dismay that it was almost on its last legs.

Every seam was beginning to fray, and there were marks under the arms that no amount of cleaning and ironing could quite erase.

"I shall have to give up my flat," she thought.

She remembered the awful discomfort of the mews where she had lodged, the noise and the terrible feeling of being surrounded by other people.

She loved the solitude and sense of private ownership which her little flat gave her, and she knew that she would rather go almost entirely without food than give up this oasis, to which she always returned with pride.

"I wonder if other people appreciate where they live, as much as I do," she thought. "Perhaps they have never known anything different. Jim's flat, for instance, luxurious, comfortable, and every beauty possible for man.

"Jim, Jim!" she whispered to herself.

She wondered if he was feeling as miserable without her as she was without him. Yet that would be his only misery.

He would not have the anxiety of food, of clothes, of

wondering whether to-night would be the last night in his job.

The fear of not pleasing, the grind of having to be everlastingly charming, cheerful, bright and alert however one was feeling inwardly, having to act and act well, because if one did not one was likely to become destitute.

Perhaps now Jim was dressing, after a bath drawn for him by his valet, his clothes laid out ready, clothes from Savile Row. Had he left now, on his way to dinner? Was he thinking of her?

Maybe—but at the same time it was very likely that he had arranged to dine with friends to-night. So easy to forget for a little while, if one could go to friends one had known since childhood, dine in their house, a marvellous dinner, good wines.

"Oh, Jim, how I want you—just for yourself, not even for your comforts. Even so, I wish I had your comforts to comfort me!"

She gave a little sob.

"I love you . . . I love you," she whispered desparingly.

CHAPTER THREE

Fiona found her new dress, and the first night she wore it was to remain indelibly in her mind for the rest of her life.

It was a black dress, very plainly cut, in chiffon, with a tiny fichu frill hung about her shoulders.

She looked particularly lovely in it, and it framed her fair hair and perfect complexion, showing them off to their very best advantage.

She arrived at Paglioni's pleased with her appearance. A week had passed slowly since she last saw Jim, so slowly that it seemed to her years and years since she had heard his voice.

Donald had managed to give her ten shillings when his wages came in, she had received a tip of ten shillings, and for twenty-five shillings she had found this dress in a little shop off Shaftesbury Avenue.

It was a bargain, the woman who sold it told Fiona, and she realised it was herself.

It was cheap because it was very slight, but Fiona managed to pull it round her, even though some of the hooks were slightly strained.

"This ought to please Paglioni," she thought as she dressed.

When she arrived he walked towards her.

"You are to dine with Lord Winthrop to-night," he said curtly. "You have a new dress—good. It was about time. I was going to speak to you about it."

He walked away, leaving Fiona with a restricted feeling in her heart, all the pleasure of her new dress gone.

"Dine with Lord Winthrop."

So he was back and she had to talk with that horrible old man again.

She walked to her table. Clare looked up at her, and said,

"Coo-oo, glum as usual. Do you ever look cheerful these days, Fiona?"

"I've got to dine with Lord Winthrop to-night," Fiona said as she sat down.

She suddenly felt faint and she beckoned the *maître-d'hôtel* as he passed.

"Could I have a cup of coffee?" she asked.

"I'm busy," he said.

Then, moved by her air of exhaustion, he ordered it for her.

When it came, it revived Fiona a little, but she still felt rather limp and shaky about the legs, as she rose to walk across the room to Lord Winthrop's table.

Luckily he was very interested in his food. He was well known as a great epicure and a connoisseur of wines, so that for the first ten minutes she was allowed to remain silent while he consulted the menu with Paglioni himself, and ordered both red and white wines of respected vintage.

"A glass of sherry?" he asked Fiona, "or would you prefer a cocktail?"

Fiona, knowing her cue that she must drink "what the client drinks," asked for sherry.

It was perhaps lucky that she did, for the small glassful went to her head a little, as she had not touched any food that day.

At last his Lordship had ordered, and turned his attention to Fiona.

"Well, my dear," he said, "are you glad to see me?"

"Of course," Fiona said, trying to smile, and succeeding faintly.

"Good, and I hope you have missed me a little."

"Of course," Fiona said again.

"Tell me what you have been doing," he said, slipping slowly at his sherry.

Fiona had a wild desire to tell him the truth.

"Supposing," she thought, "I blurted out that I had been terribly in love, had one moment's complete happiness, then had lost everything that mattered to me in my life!

"Oh, Jim, Jim!" her heart called out, and then contracted at the sight of Lord Winthrop's face near to hers.

His hand was reaching out to touch hers for a moment under the table, his knees edging against her knees.

She realised that he was waiting for her to speak, and also that unless she could keep the subject from herself his advances would become more and more undefeatable.

She plunged into a garbled account of the extraordinary people who had come from the North and danced with her there several evenings ago.

She chattered away, but knew that Lord Winthrop was not interested.

His dinner was hardly over before he said something which really frightened Fiona.

"You must allow me to come and see your little flat," he said. "I have a little present to make you for your home. A rug, my dear. A rather nice Persian one, but I must see that it will fit into your abode."

Fiona felt in a quandary. If she refused point-blank, she knew there would be a scene, and that Lord Winthrop would be angry.

If she said "thank you," he would think that she had accepted. She tried to say that she had everything she wanted, but Lord Winthrop would not listen.

"Nonsense, nonsense," he said, "a Persian rug is always an asset, and can always be put somewhere. You are not going to tell me that your place is filled with rugs."

He hesitated over the word "rugs," and Fiona guessed he was going to say "valuable rugs," and she knew that he saw through her evasion.

"Then that's settled, my dear," he said. "I will come this evening—why not? No time is better than the present, eh?"

He rose from his seat and invited her to dance; holding her tightly to him, they moved slowly and quite smoothly over the floor.

"You are looking very lovely to-night," he said. "I like your dress; it's very smart, my dear. I wonder who is the lucky man who is allowed to pay for it."

"I am not in the habit of accepting presents of clothes from men," Fiona said sharply.

"Come, come," he said, "what is the harm? You accept cheques, and gloves, or even silk stockings. You might even stretch a point and accept a little article of jewellery. Where is the difference between that and a dress?"

"I am afraid I don't get the opportunity of accepting any of those things," Fiona tried to say lightly.

Then she realised it was quite the wrong thing to have said.

"But you do! I am only too willing to give you anytihng that you need in that line, provided that you let me come with you to choose it. There is nothing I enjoy more than taking a pretty woman shopping."

He smirked a little as he said it, which made Fiona inclined to shudder.

"Well, let me tell you," she said, "that I am one of those fortunate people who have everything they want."

"Everything?" said Lord Winthrop, surprised.

As they returned to their table and sat down, he picked up her handbag, frayed, damaged and already threadbare.

The clasp was broken; Fiona had tried to hold it together with a little black cotton; inside, the white lining was stained and damaged by lipstick beyond hope of cleaning or repair.

Lord Winthrop put it down and said,

"I will give you another one to-morrow, my dear, and we will go and choose it together after lunch, eh?"

"But really," Fiona began,

Then she stopped! After all, what was the use of expostulating!

If he meant to behave like this, he would, and no amount of protestation or argument from her was going to prevent it.

He held the trump card, her job and her safety from starvation were in his hands, if he but knew it. He had only to complain, and she would be back in the street again without a job and without food.

It was not a pleasant prospect, and for the moment it beat her. Even her courage could not hold out against such possibilities.

"Why should a girl be crucified because she has no money?" Fiona thought bitterly. "It is unfair. It is bad enough not to have any means of keeping oneself without work, but because one works one is allowed to have no morals and no choice of behaviour!"

She looked at all the beautiful young débutantes and well-fed young married women who were sitting round the room.

"They don't have these problems," she thought.

Lord Winthrop took Fiona's hand under the table, and caressed it gently, moving his long fingers against her wrist, against the ball of her thumb, between her fingers.

The mere touch of him made her squirm, made her long to cry out, to hit him, to run away, to cry.

To do anything rather than sit with a smile upon her face, knowing that however much he seemed unconscious of their presence, Paglioni was watching her as a cat watches a mouse.

Lord Winthrop made love to her, all in that rather peculiar talking-down-to-a-woman way which was part of his reputation.

It was only eleven o'clock when he rose to his feet, and said, "Let me take you home."

Hostesses were not allowed to leave the restaurant until it closed, but Lord Winthrop was a law unto himself, and Fiona meekly went to get her shabby black coat from the cloakroom.

They were bowed into the Rolls-Royce waiting outside, and while they went smoothly down Piccadilly towards Chelsea, Fiona endured his kisses silently, scheming wildly for a way to prevent his coming into her flat.

She was frightened, terribly frightened, and it seemed to her he was a monster sucking her further and further into his clutches.

Everything before her was black and terrifying.

"How can I get away?" "How can I leave him?" "How can I escape?"

Her brain thought of this and that, but not clearly— as if in a fog, through which she could only grope helplessly.

Lord Winthrop held her tighter and tighter. She could feel his hand moving over her dress underneath her coat.

Suddenly the car stopped, and she lay back, dazed and shaking a little from his proximity. The chauffeur opened the door.

"Give him your key," Lord Winthrop commanded, and, without thinking, Fiona handed over her latchkey.

The chauffeur opened the house door, and Fiona turned to say good night, but Lord Winthrop followed her out of the car.

"Good night," she said quickly, with a tremor in her voice.

She tried to say something, but words failed her, and she walked slowly up the stairs, turning on the lights as she went, followed by the footsteps of Lord Winthrop.

As he put out his arms and drew Fiona into them Lord Winthrop said thickly:

"At last!"

He covered her face with kisses. Fiona tore herself away from him.

"Wait, wait," she said, "I want to show you my . . . my flat. I . . ."

She was voiceless, but it was no use talking. He moved towards her again, drew her back into his arms.

"Now you're going to be a nice girl, and let me love you," he said, caressing her.

"No, please no," Fiona said, and again tried to pull herself free.

Lord Winthrop was a strong man. He picked her up in his arms and carried her protesting into the bedroom, and put her down on the bed.

She lay for a moment panting under his kisses, then she strove madly to push him away. She succeeded, and sprang to her feet. Suddenly she felt desperate.

All ideas she had ever had of trying to placate this man, of staving him off, went out of her mind.

She did not care for anything, except that she must escape, must get away from him, must prevent him from touching her, whatever the cost, whatever happened.

No monetary advantage, no job could possibly have weighed in the balance against this violation of every feeling she had ever had.

"Go away!" she said, "Go away!"

She fled frightened across the room to stand trembling against the wall.

He went towards her and caught her, but again she escaped him, but in trying to prevent her he caught at her dress, and ripped the scarf from her shoulder.

Then the last vestige of self-control left her. She felt that she was being caught—that here was an animal, a monster of beastliness, striving to conquer and possess her.

She screamed, and as he approached her, hit out with all her force. Her clenched fist caught him in the face, and as he moved his head to avoid it, his foot slipped on the linoleum, which Fiona had polished that morning.

He turned to catch at a chair to save himself, but missed it and fell with a frightful crash to the floor.

For a moment he lay still, and then rose to his feet, crimson in the face, and obviously in a furious temper.

"You little devil!" he said thickly, and glared at her for a moment.

Then suddenly, before Fiona's horrified eyes, he

clutched at his throat, and a strange choking sound came from his chest.

He staggered back a foot or two, then sank into the armchair, still gurgling with a horrible, suffocating sound, his eyes bulged, his face contorted.

Slowly he became rigid, his hands outstretched, his mouth twisted at the side of his face, his eyes horribly staring.

For a moment he had a spasm of convulsion, and then he was still, his legs stretched stiffly before him.

Fiona stood gazing at him, paralysed with terror.

How long she stood there she did not know. She felt as though her whole body had suddenly turned to lead, and she could not move or cry out or even walk forward to see if she could do anything for him.

He lay quite still.

At last she heard hammering, something thumping, and realised it was her own heart. She began to shake all over; beads of perspiration stood on her forehead, yet she was so cold her teeth were chattering.

"What shall I do? What shall I do?" she thought wildly.

She went quite near to him, but could not bring herself to touch him.

Then she thought of the chauffeur, and pulling open her front door she ran down the stairs, nearly tripping over her dress and falling headlong.

However, the banister rails saved her, and she reached the front door. She dragged it open, to find the chauffeur had made himself comfortable and had fallen into a light slumber.

He was evidently used to long waits.

"Come up quickly!" Fiona cried breathlessly. "Help Lord Winthrop—he's ill."

The chauffeur hurried out of the car and ran up the stairs in front of Fiona three at a time. She followed as quickly as she could, her heart beating wildly, her breath coming in quick gasps.

The chauffeur was already kneeling on the floor beside his Master.

"He's all right," the chauffeur said. "He's alive but I think he's had a stroke. Got a telephone?"

Fiona shook her head.

"No."

"Oh, hell!" The chauffeur pushed his cap back from his forehead. "I'd better get him out of here. He can't be found in this sort of place. I'll take him round to the doctor myself. What the devil have you done to him, anyway?"

He gave Fiona a calculating look, and she knew that he thought she was a prostitute, but she was too upset to worry what he believed.

"How shall we get him to the car?" she asked.

"You take his legs," the chauffeur commanded, "and I'll get him under the arms. It's better to move him. If he dies it won't look well either, caught in a room with you."

Fiona said nothing. She took a safety-pin and pinned up her dress, so that it was nearly up to her knees.

Then she picked up Lord Winthrop's ankles as the chauffeur lifted him up under the arms. She went first, and started down the stairs.

He was a very heavy man, and it was with tremendous difficulty that they managed to move him. Fiona was exhausted by the time they reached the bottom.

They laid him down for a moment while the chauffeur went to open the car door. He came back in a moment and they carried the body across the pavement and lifted it on to the floor of the car.

The chauffeur got in, and managed to hoist Lord Winthrop on to the back seat. Luckily there were few people about at that hour of night.

The chauffeur shut the door, got in the front seat, and without a word to Fiona drove away.

Fiona stood on the pavement watching the car out of sight. Her arms were aching, and when she touched her hair it was damp with sweat.

She shivered—she went in, closed the door and climbed upstairs. There for a long time she stood with her hands over her aching eyes.

Her bed was crumpled where Lord Winthrop had lain her on it, chairs were overturned and everything looked untidy, and to her unpleasant.

Her head was throbbing with a painfulness that was terrifying.

"I feel as though I'm going mad!" Fiona muttered to herself.

She felt that at any moment she was going to be sick. She walked up and down the room, wringing her hands, damp and cold.

"What a terrible thing to happen . . . Why should it happen to me? . . . Thank God he was out of here! Yet supposing he dies, there will be an inquest . . .

"Will the chauffeur say that he found him already laying back . . . half-dead when he came up here, or will he lie . . . and say he had a . . . stroke in the car? Shall I be . . . dragged into this!"

At last she could bear it no longer. She could not undress and go into her room—the crumpled bed gave her too vivid recollections of what had passed.

She put on her black coat and went into the street.

She walked aimlessly for a long while, the cool air on her cheeks helping to ease a little her throbbing head, and then she realised she was walking in the direction of Park Lane.

She finally came to a stop outside Winthrop House. It was a large, gaunt mansion, white and forbidding, with a low wall surrounding the small garden.

There were no signs of activity in the house, but while she stood there looking at it, wondering what was happening inside, a car drove up and a man with a bag stepped out of it and rang the bell.

Almost immediately it was opened. A specialist, Fiona thought. She stood there a long time, and eventually a taxi arrived, and a nurse got out.

"He's obviously alive," she thought. "He's alive . . . but I wonder if he will . . . remember what . . . happened?"

She heard a clock strike five o'clock, and she turned

and walked away down Park Lane, which was quite deserted.

Of a sudden she realised she was very, very cold, and very, very tired. The early morning air was chilly and damping, and her coat afforded her little protection.

It took her half an hour to get back to Chelsea.

She was so cold and miserable that she did not feel even upset at the thought of her room, and the untidiness meant nothing to her brain, which had become as numbed as her body.

When finally she crept between the sheets she was shivering all over, and she could not sleep, though her eyes closed from sheer utter fatigue. She could not think.

She just seemed to be drifting in a void, in which there was no coherence. She heard the traffic rumbling down King's Road, and she lay for a long time like one unconscious, but never asleep.

At last she felt a warmth on her cheeks, and opened her eyes to find the sun was shining through the window she had forgotten to fasten.

"Sunshine!" she thought. "What have I got to do with sunshine?"

As her circulation began to revive, she found that she was aching all over with a dull, agonising ache that grew worse instead of better as the morning proceeded.

When she got up to boil a kettle to make herself a cup of tea, she found that she could hardly stand.

"This is . . . nonsense," she said to herself; "you must control yourself . . . it is only nerves."

But nevertheless, it was with great difficulty that she crossed the tiny room, turned on the gas-ring and placed the kettle upon it.

"I can't be ill," she thought, angry with herself. "It is absurd! I've got to go out and get some food, and I have got to be well enough to go to . . . Paglioni's to-night."

The thought of that made her shudder, and sent a quivering fear all over her.

Supposing this morning Lord Winthrop was dead?

Would she be cross-examined as the last person to see him? What would the chauffeur say?

Fear was suggesting all sorts of things to her, and her imagination endowed them with the reality which her common sense could not combat.

Finally, aching in every limb, she dressed herself and went into the street to buy bread, margarine and two eggs—all she could afford, for she knew that she had only seven shillings and sixpense to last her to the end of the week.

In a fit of economy, she had given up milk in her tea, and had taken to drinking the strong mixture without anything save sugar to relieve it.

But to-day she was extravagant and bought half a pint of fresh milk from the dairy.

Home again, she felt so exhausted and ill that she beat up one of her precious eggs in the milk and drank it off.

She could not face the thought of having to clean her room, a task in which she usually took much pride.

Without taking off her coat, she laid down on her unmade bed and closed her eyes. She was haunted by the thought of Lord Winthrop. It was impossible to rest.

"Is he alive, or is he dead?"

It became like a childish nursery rhyme repeating itself over and over again in her head;

"Is he alive or is he dead? Is he alive or is he dead?"

At last, as though compelled by some force stronger than herself, she went down the stairs and out along the road to a public telephone box.

She entered it, turned over the pages of the book until she found "Winthrop," and asked for the number. It seemed ages before she could press Button A.

"Hullo, hullo."

The voice sounded curt and hurried.

"Can you tell me how Lord Winthrop is?" Fiona asked.

"Who is that speaking?" said the voice.

"He's not dead . . . tell me," Fiona said, losing her head.

There was a short silence, as if of surprise.

"Certainly not. Who is that speaking?"

But Fiona had heard all she wanted to, and she put down the receiver. He wasn't dead . . . that was all that mattered. She went home quickly, and already her step lighter and more buoyant.

She made herself another cup of tea, and then, utterly exhausted, got into bed. She was aroused hours later by knocking at the door, and opened it to find Donald.

"How late you are, Fiona," he said, as she let him in.

"I was rather late last night," Fiona replied.

She flushed as she spoke, but Donald did not notice it.

"My brother has been turned out," he said abruptly, standing in the center of the room.

"Oh, Donald, I am sorry." Fiona forgot her own troubles for the moment, and went forward to him with outstretched hands.

Donald paid no attention to her. He was looking across the room, out through the window at the housetops of Chelsea, and his hands were clenched at his sides.

"He couldn't put it back cleverly enough," he said hoarsely. "He wasn't cut out to be a crook. He was only a fool, and not a clever fool at that."

"They haven't sent him to prison?" Fiona asked quickly.

"No, they haven't done that," Donald said, "not yet, but they may. We don't know. Your money may save him. They have dismissed him, of course. We shall know what they're going to do about it later.

"I have taken your money, and I can't get it back. And it may be ages before I can return it. I have got to keep the boy as well as myself now, you see.

"However carefully we go I shan't be able to pay you back much for some time, unless, of course, a miracle happens."

"That's all right, Donald, don't worry. I shall manage," Fiona said.

"Fiona, you're a brick." Donald cheered up for the

moment. He put out his hand and patted her arm. "I can't thank you enough—I never can. You know how much it means to me to have you stand by me even apart from the money.

"You know I love you, Fiona. I have done so for a long time. This isn't the moment to tell you if I hadn't need to, but I do, Fiona, I love you with all my heart and soul."

The sincerity in his voice and the fervour of it suddenly made Fiona feel very weak. She sat down in a chair.

"That's all right, Donald, but please don't let's talk about it for the moment. I am tired, terribly tired."

"Fiona, you're ill—why didn't you tell me? What's the matter, dear? What has happened to you?"

Fiona shook her head.

"Nothing," she said, "just nothing. Leave me alone."

Donald had the sense to do as he was told. He saw she was very near tears, and he turned away towards the window. He lit a cigarette, and gave Fiona time to control herself.

But when he looked round again he was genuinely alarmed by her pallor and her look of complete exhaustion.

"I am going out to get you something to drink," he said. "Don't argue. For one thing, it will pull you together. I shan't be long. Sit still till I come back." He took a bottle from the cupboard and went down the stairs.

As soon as the echo of his footsteps had died away, Fiona lay back and closed her eyes. Everything was going round and round in a big circle.

"It's just weakness," she told herself, "just shock."

But she knew that she must have caught a chill last night.

It seemed a long time to her before she heard Donald returning. He came in with his arms laden with parcels.

First, he put a shilling in the gas meter, then he

produced the bottle filled with whisky. He had bought, too, some sausages and potatoes.

"I am going to cook you a proper meal," he said. "I know you had nothing for lunch, so it's no use your telling me you had."

"I wonder where he got the money," Fiona thought quickly, and then she cried out: "Where's your overcoat, Donald?"

He had gone out in a cheap tweed overcoat. His suit was threadbare, but his overcoat was quite good-looking, and he had told Fiona that it was probably his chief asset, and he always kept it on, as it made him look less shabby.

"Lovely warm weather," Donald said, busy over the gas-ring.

Fiona cried out,

"Oh, Donald, you shouldn't—you know you shouldn't!"

"If you think I'm going to let you starve yourself while I walk about overheated, you're mistaken," Donald said with a smile, and Fiona could have cried at his kindness.

She felt disinclined for food, but realised that to please Donald she must eat the sausages. When they came sizzling from the hearth with chipped potatoes beside them, she found they were delicious, and moreover that she was very hungry indeed.

When she had finished, Donald said to her:

"Now go and get into bed. You will be able to have a good sleep before you go out to work. I am going to make you a hot toddy. I'll bring it to you in exactly three minutes."

Like a child she obeyed him, she was far too tired to argue and it was a joy for some one to take command and make her do what he wanted.

She hurried into her bedroom and got straight into bed, but she was hardly settled down before there was a knock on the door and Donald came in with a steaming glass in his hand.

Piping hot, the whisky made very strong, it was nice,

with the lemon and the sugar in it. Fiona felt it burn down her throat, warming her as it went.

"Must I drink it all?" she asked.

"Every drop," Donald said.

She knew he was right, and that it would do her good. She felt a delicious warmth creeping over her. The whisky went to her head a little. She felt drowsy and slightly drunk.

Donald drew the curtains, and then with a motherly touch bent down and tucked in her feet.

"Sleep well," he said. "I'll come back about nine o'clock, in case you have slept as late as that, and we can go up together in the 'bus."

"Thank you, Donald dear," Fiona murmured, half asleep already. She heard him moving in the next room, and then she slipped into a deep, dreamless slumber.

When she awoke her clock told her that it was after eight. She got up, went into the next room, and was very moved by what she saw. Donald had put everything ready for her to have a bath.

She had purchased some time ago, for a few odd shillings, an old, rather chipped hip-bath in the King's Road; her largest kettle filled twice would make enough water for it when the cold was added.

Now on the hearth the kettle was waiting for her, the gas turned low under it.

On the table the things were laid for a cup of tea, and a ham sandwich was already cut daintily inviting for her. Propped against the teapot was:

"Eat this as soon as you wake up. Love, D."

"Dear Donald! How kind you are to me." She smiled, her misery evaporated by his sweetness.

She did as she was told, ate the one sandwich and had a cup of tea, then got into her bath.

"There is nothing more marvellous than a hot bath when one is tired," she said to herself.

Fiona lingered until the water began to get cold, then she got out feeling refreshed and much better. She dressed, and put on her old red chiffon—she could not face the memories of last night with her new frock with its torn fichu.

"If I were rich," she though ruefully, "I'd burn that frock. I think it's unlucky. But I am poor, to-morrow I shall spend a long time mending it, and then I shall wear it so often that there will be lots of pleasant memories to replace the unpleasant ones."

When Donald arrived at nine o'clock she was ready for him, and was busily engaged cooking the rest of the sausages and breaking her only remaining egg into a delicious concoction which was half an omelette and half scrambled eggs.

She knew that Donald would have spent his last penny on her, without a doubt having every intention of going to work at his office with an empty stomach.

She did not mean him to do so, for the mere thought of him without his overcoat in the cold night air brought tears to her eyes.

"I'm so much better, thanks to you," she told Donald gaily as he arrived. "You've been an angel to me. Now sit down and see if I'm as good a cook as you!"

He complimented her by eating every morsel of the food, though he insisted on her sharing it with him, although she protested she was having a big supper later.

"You look half starved," he said severely. "If you go on like this, Fiona, you'll lose your looks, and that will mean you'll lose your job."

'I nearly lost it through my looks,' Fiona thought to herself, but she said nothing to Donald.

"What about your brother?" she asked.

"I've left him at home," he said. "He's going to stay with me for a bit, he doesn't dare face Mother.

"She is so proud of him being in an office in the City. She rather looks down on journalism, thinks it isn't steady, and she likes having the youngest in what she calls 'a respectable job.'

"He has written to her that he is doing overtime, and is going to stay with me while the hours are so late. When he finds something else, he can go back.

"As a matter of fact, he can't raise the fare at the

66

moment, it's ninepence each way, you know, on the Underground. Oh, Fiona, you don't know what you've saved us all from!"

"Now look here, Donald," Fiona said. "I'm not going to allow you to talk about it any more. Please, please treat that subject as one that is never to be mentioned by us, ever."

Donald held out his hands; she put hers into them.

"Thank you, my darling," he said very gently, and gravely.

They lingered so long talking that they were almost late, and had to run to catch the 'bus which was to carry them to their destinations.

"Good night," Fiona smiled, as she rose at her stopping place.

Donald watched her as she got down and crossed the road. The 'bus jolted on, and she was lost in the darkness.

Fiona hurried into Paglioni's. It was on the stroke of ten as she arrived, so she could not waste much time in the cloakroom.

She hung up her coat, and hurried through the lounge into the restaurant.

She saw Paglioni coming across the lounge towards her, then just before he reached her he picked up a paper from his desk.

"Good evening, Mr. Paglioni," she faltered.

"Do you know anything about this?" he asked.

She saw the heading of the *Evening Standard* that he carried.

Her startled eyes read: *"Famous Peer Dead"*.

Then the print swam before her, the music in the distance faded away, and with a cry she collapsed in a faint at Paglioni's feet.

* * *

Fiona came round to find herself in Jim's arms.

For a moment she lay there limply against his shoul-

67

der, thinking that she was dreaming, and on her way to Heaven.

Then she heard his dear voice say, "Drink this," and felt the brandy burn itself down her throat.

"Jim?" she said weakly.

"Yes, me." He smiled back at her. "Are you all right now?"

She was sitting on the sofa in the room upstairs which was sometimes used for private dinner-parties.

"Darling, what have you been doing to yourself? What has happened?" Jim asked her. "Why are you looking so ill?"

For a few seconds Fiona was content to rest her head against his shoulder, and not answer. She no longer felt faint, the brandy had done its work, but instead she felt warm and weary, in a cosy, drifting way.

"Jim," she kept thinking to herself, "Jim—my own Jim!"

At last she raised her face to his.

"Why are you here?" she said.

He got up, and letting her sink carefully back against the cushions, lifted her feet to the ground and then, half-sitting, half-kneeling, at her side he took her cold hands in his and gently rubbed them.

"I didn't mean to come here, Fiona," he said at last. "I arranged to dine with some friends of mine. I had no idea they were going to choose Paglioni's, but when I arrived at their house for a cocktail, they told me it was all fixed up and ordered, and I couldn't very well fail them like that at the last moment, so I came along."

He paused.

"Thank God, I did! We had finished dinner, and I guessed you would be arriving, so I walked outside in the hope of seeing you for a moment. I didn't want you to be upset at seeing me in the restaurant.

"I saw you faint. It gave me such a shock, Fiona! Darling, I love you more than ever. I've never been through such an awful moment as when you collapsed."

His voice deepened.

"I didn't know what had happened—you just fell.

Tell me—tell me what has happened to you. Why do you look so ill, Fiona, what have you been doing to yourself?"

Haltingly, hesitatingly, Fiona told him everything. He did not interrupt her, save to murmur once or twice, unconsciously clenching his fists.

When she had finished, Fiona lay there weakly, and slowly the tears forced their way under closed eyes and ran down her white cheeks.

Jim watched her for a moment in silence, then he rose to his feet.

"I'm going to telephone," he said casually. "You are not to move till I come back."

"But Jim—" she expostulated, starting to get up.

He pressed her back again, in a masterful way that she loved.

"You heard what I said," he said gently, "you're to stay here till I come back. I have plans. Now, don't interrupt me, my sweet."

He disappeared, and Fiona lay back, her weary limbs relaxing against the softness of the cushions.

She was deliciously content to do as Jim told her, to be under his orders, to know that he was seeing after her, and that he was there, for the moment anyway, to love and cherish her.

"Jim! Jim!" she murmured to herself, and raised the hand, that he had held, against her cheek.

"I love him," she thought, "I love him."

Five minutes later he returned.

"It's all arranged, darling," he said. "You're coming away to-night, and you're going to have a real rest in the country."

"In the country?" Fiona said, startled.

"I'm going to take you to stay with some very old friends of mine," he said. "They are charming people, very quiet, but very sweet, and they will look after you."

"But Paglioni—" Fiona said. "He will never allow me to go."

"He most certainly will," Jim answered. "I'm going

to speak to that gentleman. It's half his fault that all this has happened."

"Please . . . please, Jim," Fiona begged, "I shall lose my job, and it's so impossible to get another one. Please don't be difficult."

"I won't," Jim promised her. "I'll fix it, darling, so that it will be quite all right, but you're to do as I tell you. You've got to have a rest. I will take a week's leave to be with you. Stay here."

Again he disappeared, and returned with Paglioni, who was bowing and smiling and apparently quite well-pleased that his arrangements should be upset, or rather rearranged for him by this impulsive young man.

He told Fiona that she could certainly have a week's leave, and though she had a suspicion that perhaps Jim had paid him to allow her this, she was too tired and too weary to ask any questions.

He helped her downstairs and insisted on wrapping her up in his own big fur-lined coat, so as not to catch cold in the open car.

He was driving himself, as he so often did, and they went first to his flat where he kept her waiting for a few moments while he got his suitcase and another coat for himself.

At Chelsea, he did all the running about, even insisting on packing for her, putting her things in all wrong, but determined that she should not exert herself in any way.

"Who said I wouldn't make a good lady's-maid?" he asked laughing, as he pressed the last dress into the papier mache suitcase and clipped down the catches, "or rather a good husband?"

"Don't, Jim," Fiona whispered. "Don't joke about it, darling . . . I can't bear it."

"Oh, my sweet!" Jim put his arms round her. "It's a damnable joke, I agree. I can't bear it, Fiona, either. I want you so."

He kissed her mouth and the top of her neck which was just showing above the dark fastening of her coat, then he let her go, and in silence they went downstairs to the car.

Fiona had written a short note to Donald, and she pinned it on the door outside her flat, so that he would know she was all right, although Jim would not tell her the address of where she was going to.

"I don't want you to be disturbed by anybody." he said. "I want you to have a complete rest, away from all worries."

They were very soon out of London, and the smell of the countryside greeted her like a long-lost friend.

At last Jim turned off into a narrow, unevenly surfaced lane. At the end of it, they came to a tiny black-and-white lodge with a thatched roof, the entrance to a narrow, tree-bordered drive which brought them to the house.

As Jim switched off the engine, there was the barking of dogs, a door opened and the light streamed out to them.

In the doorway stood a tall, good-looking man of about sixty, and a moment later he was joined by his wife, young-looking but grey-haired.

"Jim, darling, how thrilling to see you!" she exclaimed, and kissed him on both cheeks. "And this is your friend."

She held out a hand to Fiona.

There are some people whom one takes an instantaneous liking to, and Mrs. Carey was one of them.

She was so very lovely, in a natural and unartificial manner, and she had an enchanting friendliness about her which contained no hint of condescension or patronage, just genuine delight at making a new acquaintance.

Not the least part of her charm was her tremendous happiness because of her love for her husband.

Mr. Carey helped Fiona out of the car.

"Come into the warm," he said, "you must be frozen."

"I'm not," Fiona laughed, as he tried to extricate her from the folds of two or three rugs and the heavy coat that weighed her down.

She entered the house, and was led to a roaring fire in the big, oak-panelled sitting-room.

Sandwiches were handed to her, and Jim insisted on her having a brandy and soda.

While the Careys talked, evidently very glad to see Jim again, Fiona looked from one to the other, trying to take in a quick impression of what was before her for the next week.

She decided that she would most certainly enjoy herself, and then, to her horror, she found herself almost falling asleep over the fireside.

The drink and the warmth, after the cold and the trouble she had been through, were too much for her.

"Bless us, the child is nearly asleep!" exclaimed Mrs. Carey. "Come along, my dear—I will show you your room, and you must jump into bed just as quickly as you can."

Upstairs a maid had already finished unpacking, a large fire was burning on the hearth, and a comfortable bed with soft, lavender-scented sheets was very inviting.

In five minutes Fiona was ready, and as she slipped between the sheets she thought:

"This is all a dream, it cannot be true. This cannot be me, Fiona, who only last night was miserable in Chelsea."

As she stretched out her hand to switch off the lamp by her bedside, there was a quiet knock and Jim put his head round the door.

"Are you all right?" he asked.

"I'm very happy," Fiona answered.

He came across the room to her.

"Good night, my darling. Sleep well. I'm so terribly happy to be with you again."

He kissed her forehead, and then, after hesitating a moment as if he longed to kiss her again, he walked back to the door.

"Good night, my Fiona," he whispered, and shutting the door very quietly behind him, was gone.

Fiona switched off the light, and a few moments later her even breathing was the only sound in the room.

*　　*　　*

Jim's heart called out to Fiona, but his honour and all his training made him know that, however much he loved Fiona, his allegiance and loyalty must be to Ann.

Every day and every evening he had had to battle with himself not to go and see Fiona; to fight against the desire to look at her, to see her if only for one moment.

He was in love, so madly that it was with difficulty he could control his feelings and his conversation to any semblance of naturalness with those around him.

His best friends were mystified, even his acquaintances were surprised.

"What's the matter with Jim?" they asked each other. "Seems a bit queer these days."

They did not know that Jim was almost gripping the sides of his chair to keep his feet from carrying him swiftly towards the gaily lighted door of Paglioni's.

At night he could not sleep. A vision of Fiona haunted him, and he would spend hours walking up and down his bedroom, or he would take his car and drive out into the country, to return only as dawn was breaking.

"What am I to do? What am I to do?" he asked himself at last. "I want Fiona—she wants me. And yet my duty is to Ann. I cannot let her down."

Although Fiona slept peacefully that night in a strange house, Jim lay wakeful, his brain revolving ceaselessly in a circle from which there seemed no escape.

In the morning Fiona woke, to sunshine streaming through the chintz-curtained windows and breakfast in bed.

"What fun!" she thought to herself, as the tray, with its lace-edged white cloth and service of buttercup-yellow, was brought to her bedside.

The scrambled eggs were hot under a shining silver cover, four pieces of toast invited her appetite with marmalade or jam to spread on them.

A small bunch of grapes and an apple were also on the tray.

Fiona did full justice to the meal for she finished everything, even to emptying the pot of coffee.

As she finished, the maid knocked at the door.

"Would you like your bath now, miss," she asked, "or will you wait for a little while?"

"Now, please," Fiona answered, eager to be up and to see everything, and more eager—though she would not own it to herself—to see Jim.

After a delightful bath Fiona stood hesitating for a moment, trying to screw up her courage to go downstairs.

"I wonder where they will be," she thought to herself. "I do hope they won't think I look awful."

As she hesitated she heard a gay whistle outside, and her name called. Opening the long window which led onto a stone balcony, she stepped out into the sunshine, and there below her stood Jim.

"Come down," he said, "quickly, darling—I've got lots to show you!"

Fiona smiled, and waved her hand.

"I'm coming!" she cried.

CHAPTER FOUR

Happy days pass too quickly even for memory.

Love makes an hour into a minute, a day into a moment as swift in passage as a kiss.

Fiona laughed with Jim, walked with him, watched him play golf, drove to the sea and bathed with him; they picnicked in the woods, they looked into each other's eyes and sighed; and a week passed.

The weather was glorious. The Careys, in the knowledge of their own happiness, were perfect chaperones. There was only one cloud to shadow and frighten Fiona —the imminence of her return to London.

She heard no more of Lord Winthrop; she read of his funeral, attended by a very large number of friends, and that the King was represented.

Jim forbade her to think about it; in fact, he was very arbitrary about her thinking of or discussing anything which concerned the past or the future.

"Let's be happy together, dear," he said. "What does it matter now, this moment, what troubles to-morrow may bring? Don't frown, Fiona—kiss me!"

Fiona kissed him lightly, but in a moment his arms were around her, holding her close, and again closer to him. His kiss seemed to draw her heart from her body.

She felt herself tremble, and her eyes close. She was in a dream, enveloped in a warm happiness, from which she prayed there was no awakening.

Then suddenly Jim took his arms from her, so suddenly that she kept her balance only by putting out her hand and holding the trunk of a fir tree.

With his back to her, he was looking at the view, the valley below, its tiny houses, red-roofed, dotted about like mushrooms, its profusion of green with a small river winding like a lazy silver snake through the fields.

Fiona watched him. She loved the sunshine on his fair hair, the bright sunburn of his neck above his collar, the broad shoulders squared as though he faced the world, antagonistic.

Tears smarted in Fiona's eyes, she felt them warm and wet on her cheeks, and she was blinded by them on her lashes.

"Jim," she said brokenly, and once again the haven of his arms soothed her.

"Darling, darling!" he murmured again and again, his cheek against hers, but he did not kiss her.

Soon she was smiling, laughing with him, but the cloud was there in the blue of her sky. In a short time they would part, and both feared that moment.

And to-day had come, her last day in the blessed peace of the sunny hills, her last day with the Careys, her last day with Jim.

She had lain awake, last night, and the joy of her visit had passed before her, a mental kaleidoscope. She experienced again each moment of wonder and gladness, each thrill of enjoyment, each heart-beat of love.

Never had she believed that love could have been such physical agony as was her love for Jim now. It was pain to be apart from him, and pain, delicious, torturing pain, to be with him.

She wanted him so, she wanted to belong to him to be his for ever, to be part of him. How could she face a future in which she was alone without him, a future lonely with an utter loneliness because she had known him?

Wild ideas, mad schemes, ran through her mind, crazy plans to hold him, to keep him. The thought of

Ann, of his marrying, was so agonising that she could not bear it.

She could not bear to think that she would never see him again, never hear his gay voice, see his smile and the look in his eyes as he held out his arms.

Never again to feel his arms around her, to smell the scent of his tweed coat, and to know that his mouth sought hers.

Jim serious, Jim gay, Jim anxious, Jim teasing, Jim loving—each mood, each expression, passed before her sleepless eyes, each picture more precious than the last, each memory a love scar which would remain with her always.

To-day the sun was shining, but its glory seemed to hold a fierce glitter as of unshed tears. Together she and Jim had picknicked under the trees.

It was very hot, and after luncheon they had lain quiet, staring at the green branches above them, listening to the birds and the gentle rustling of the forest.

There seemed so little need for words between them, they were both so much at peace together, so happy in the knowledge of each other's presence.

Hours later they wandered back to the house. The sun was sinking in a blaze of splendour over the South Downs.

Contrasting the red glory of its descent trembled the first evening star, and the moon, as yet a pale ghost, unseen, was travelling up the heavens.

Jim was shaking a cocktail as Mrs. Carey came into the room.

"Would you think us very rude," she asked, "if John and I went out to dinner? We have been asked to go to some dear friends of ours, and we would like to go, but—"

"Of course, go," Jim interrupted. "I'll look after Fiona."

"Please don't refuse because of me," Fiona begged.

Then, as Mrs. Carey left the room, her eyes met Jim's.

"What fun!" he said. "Dinner alone, sweetheart!"

She smiled at him, and as he handed her a cocktail he snatched a kiss.

Fiona lay in her bath a long time, luxuriously enjoying the warm water, the profusion of bath salts, the huge tablet of soap scented with lavender, and the large bath-sheet which awaited to dry her.

She put on her dress and took extra trouble over her face and hair. At last she was ready, and went down just as the deep-throated gong boomed its message through the house.

"Darling, you look lovely," Jim murmured as the butler left the room.

"Thank-you." Fiona whispered her reply.

Jim raised his glass.

"To the only woman I have ever loved," he said, and Fiona felt the blood thunder in her ears.

She hardly knew what she ate, she knew only that she was happy, that Jim was talking, that underneath his words his heart was calling to hers.

When they had finished coffee, he drew her from the table into the garden. In silence they walked away from the house. In the shadow of a lilac tree he took her into his arms.

"Are you mine, Fiona?" he asked as his mouth touched hers. "Do you love me?"

"More than anything in the world. I am yours, you know I am, every scrap of me."

The words burst from Fiona as if they had been pent up for ages, and she put her arms round his neck.

How long they stood there she never knew. Finally Jim picked her up as though she were a baby and carried her back to the house.

"You still weigh nothing," he said lightly, but she knew by his voice he had been profoundly stirred.

"I'm pounds heavier," she protested, laughing.

In the sitting-room he turned on the gramophone. The soft strains of a violin solo seemed to blend with the night outside and the romance between them.

For a long time they sat listening, saying nothing, and then at last Jim rose to his feet, and as though in an effort to dispel more serious things put on a record of crooning jazz.

"Come and dance, Fiona," he said, and they danced rhythmically together on the small patch of parquet floor uncovered by the rugs.

"To-morrow night I shall be dancing," she thought to herself, "and how different it will be."

She shut her eyes; her cheek was against Jim's shoulder, as they moved together in perfect unison.

What peace and happiness this was, she thought— the soft music, the quiet of the room, and the warm scented night outside the open windows.

The lights were few and shaded, but they hadn't the sinister, suggestive dimness which Paglioni cultivated to excite his clients.

"This is heaven!" she murmured, and in answer Jim put his lips against her forehead.

They danced for a long time, Jim changing the tunes —a tango, a brisk fox-trot, and an old-fashioned valse, which finished with them both flushed and laughing.

"You dance on my heart," he said and his voice was hoarse.

They sought the cool night air and yet Fiona would not wander far from the lighted windows. She did not trust herself, and did not care to test Jim's control in the purple stillness.

The dark woods tempted her, with the stars peeping through the heavy branches overhead. But some caution made her choose to sit on the little paved terrace just outside the sitting-room.

Jim lit a cigarette and moved restlessly about. Then after a moment he threw it away, and sitting down beside her took her hand in his.

"Fiona," he said softly, and she felt the atmosphere between them electric.

"Jim," she whispered.

Just for a moment her eyes held his, speaking things which she dared not say out loud. Then she rose to her feet.

"I'm going to bed, Jim," she said, a little unsteadily. "I've got so much to do to-morrow."

Her voice broke on the last words, and without further farewell she slipped away from him, and passing into the house ran upstairs.

In her bedroom, she sat on the bed and stared into space. She felt as though a great gulf, a chasm of desolation, opened before her.

It was over now, all this happiness, this week of wonderment—it was finished. To-morrow she would go back to London, back to work, and away from Jim and all that his love meant to her.

"I won't think about it," she told herself, "I must try to sleep."

But she knew that it would be an impossibility to-night. She undressed slowly, almost mechanically, and then, turning out the lights, save for the small candle-shaped one beside her bed, she drew back the taffeta curtains and opened the long French window on to the balcony.

The night invited her, and putting on her dressing-gown and bedroom slippers she stepped out and stood looking up at the stars, her hands on the cool stone balustrade.

"How small I feel," she thought, "under such a vast heaven. So small, that my troubles should not matter as they do."

But her philosophy could not prevent her tears slowly trickling down her cheeks. She heard a movement, and turned her head.

The Carey's house was built in almost Italian style. A balcony ran the whole length of the first floor, forming a verandah beneath. All the bedrooms opened on to the balcony with long French windows.

As Fiona turned now at the sound of a footfall, she saw Jim come out of his bedroom at the far end of the house.

He was smoking a cigarette, but as he saw her he threw it away, and walked very quickly towards her.

She stood perfectly still. Somehow this meeting

seemed inevitable, and as she waited for him to approach it jumped to her mind that this was meant.

That she was intended to wait for him like this, that there was some meaning in this chance encounter, after she had already left him for the night.

She raised her eyes to his as he drew near and stood quite close to her, yet not touching her. It was Jim who finally broke the silence between them, a silence pregnant with unspoken words.

"You didn't say good night to me, Fiona," he said, his voice very deep and low.

Fiona did not answer. She turned her head and looked out over the garden, so that he could only see her profile, the moonlight shining on her fair hair and catching a glint from her eyes.

"Why didn't you say good night?" Jim insisted, and he put out his hand and covered her two which lay on the balustrade.

For a moment they quivered under his touch, and Fiona was very still.

"I didn't . . . dare," she said at last, her voice hardly above a whisper.

"My darling," Jim whispered in return.

He drew her gently but firmly into his arms, but he did not kiss her.

Her heart leapt, and yet she knew that this was unwise, and that she should leave him now as she had already done a short time ago.

Yet she felt a strange lassitude which prevented her from doing anything but acquiescing to Jim's wish.

Something stronger than herself seemed to compel her to stay there in his arms.

She could not make an effort to move, she could only feel happy and utterly content, even while her pulses throbbed and the blood raced in her veins.

Slowly his hold on her tightened. She raised her face to his.

"Fiona, I love you," Jim said. "God, how I love you!"

He didn't kiss her, he only looked at her for what seemed a long time. Then he said:

"Will you live with me, my darling, so that I can look after you, at any rate until—"

He paused and they both knew what name was left unsaid. After a moment she said rather shyly:

"Should I say yes?"

"No my precious," he answered. "You shouldn't and I'm a cad to ask it of you."

"I . . . love . . . you." Fiona murmured. "I do . . . love you."

Jim took a deep breath.

"I tell you what we'll do my precious one. We will be together but I will not make you mine. I love you too much to do anything which might hurt you."

"Do you . . . mean that?" Fiona asked.

"I mean it, and I swear to you that I will take care of you and protect you, not only from the things which frighten you my darling, but from myself."

He held her closer.

"My wonderful, wonderful girl we will be together—which is all that matters."

* * *

Jim was shaving.

His mirror, adjusted on the wall, was tilted at exactly the right angle to catch the light, and his razor moved smoothly over his chin.

He was very precise and neat about the operation, and Fiona, sitting watching him, laughed, as she invariably did, at what she called his "old-maidish" methods.

"I've never met a man so particular about small things," she would tease him. "You were meant to be a crusty old bachelor, with your slippers, your pipe and your daily *Times* in exactly the same place. You certainly weren't meant to live a domestic life."

After their last night together at the Careys' house, Jim had insisted on her taking a flat with him, and not returning to Paglioni's.

Fiona was content to do as he wished, and let him run her life as he pleased.

She had not realised before how much of her dread of returning to London was the thought of her re-entrance into Paglioni's.

She had left the place that fateful night, not knowing how much or how little Paglioni knew or guessed of her association with Lord Winthrop's death. She was also terrified of facing the cross-examination from Clare and Paul.

And because her nerves were unsettled she was also dreading that corner table where Lord Winthrop had always sat.

Before she entered Paglioni's she was anticipating ghosts, and when Jim decided that she should not return, she was not only happy but relieved.

Thankfully she accepted his decision, but nevertheless she made up her mind to find work.

While she was content that Jim should pay the rent of the flat and occasionally buy her clothes, she did not intend that he should provide her with petty cash.

She could not explain her feelings over this. It was some deeply engrained, almost Puritanical streak in her, which while she could accept a home and presents from the man she loved, refused to let her look to him as a provider of commonplace expenses.

The only thing Jim stipulated was that she should not take any form of employment in a restaurant or dancing place.

"You couldn't be there in the evenings," he said. "I want you then."

As a matter of fact, had Fiona not been looking for work she would have found the days rather lonely at times, for Jim had a good many things to do, and also a good many people he was forced to see, whether he wanted to or not.

He could seldom find time to have luncheon with her, and though they were usually together uninterrupted from six onwards, in the morning and the afternoon Fiona was alone.

They were absurdly happy in the tiny service flat which Jim had taken, which was high enough to have a view of the Park and the green trees from its windows.

Fiona had never before realised what happiness could mean. She revelled in the luxury of lovely things, good furniture, fires and two baths a day.

At the same time, these superficialities were infinitesimal compared with the deep, unending joy she found in Jim's company. They were absolutely happy together.

At times, they would talk seriously for hours on end, discussing all subjects, personal and universal, subjects that were interesting to thinking men and women.

Then, without warning, Jim would become a happy schoolboy. He would tease Fiona, ruffling her hair, ragging her until she begged for mercy.

They would laugh like children, and romp until they were tired, or until their light kisses became deeper and they found themselves serious with the depth of their love.

"I love you my darling, my precious one," Jim would gasp.

His mouth would possess Fiona and she would echo this wild rapturous emotion while knowing that they must both keep an iron control on themselves.

Sometimes it was very hard and the flames within them would suddenly become a raging fire—then Jim would move away from Fiona fighting for breath.

"I'm . . . sorry," she whispered.

"Oh, my darling, I want you so desperately!" he would reply.

After a long search, Fiona found a job as dance assistant at a school of dancing. It was a large school at which every form of dancing was taught, but they required an assistant for the ball-room class.

The principal—an Italian—took Fiona on the distinct understanding that if she was unsatisfactory in any way she would have to leave, without notice or wages.

Glad to find a job of any sort, Fiona agreed, and for

the sum of twenty-five shillings a week she found herself employed every morning from eleven till one, and every afternoon from two till five. She found the work quite easy after her long hours at Paglioni's.

The season was drawing to a close and London was emptying.

Fiona had held her job for nearly three weeks when she was informed that in August the school would shut for a month, and no promise could be made that all present teachers could be re-engaged in September.

She was upset at this, because so far she and Jim had made no plans for August, and Fiona was afraid that Jim would have to go to Scotland, and that she would be alone in London, friendless and without work.

Jim, however, when she told him the news, was delighted.

"I thought we might go South, darling," he said. "I know of a little place with a tiny hotel along the Mediterranean coast some way from Cannes where we would be absolutely alone, and terribly happy."

She smiled delightedly at him.

"Oh, darling, how wonderful!" she answered. "That would be the most marvellous thing. I've always longed to go to the South of France."

Jim laughed at her ecstatic tone, and then he said seriously:

"You make everything so wonderful with your enthusiasm. Oh, my dear, I wish I could give you everything always! Why can't we be married, Fiona?

"I want you here with me, I want to take you about so that everyone can see you and admire you as I do. I hate this hole-and-corner business, this pretence to my friends."

Fiona started at his vehement tones, and stared at him as he continued, his voice low and bitter with feeling.

"Something must have upset him," she thought.

There was never any mention of Ann between them, but they both knew that she was there, in the future, ready to take Jim away and spoil the lives of them.

What had happened, Fiona wondered. Why was Jim upset? Could he have seen Ann?

A wave of jealousy swept over her at the thought, but then Jim would have told her had he done so. She put her arms round him now.

"Don't, darling," she said, "there's no point in fighting. It can't be helped, and being unhappy doesn't make it any better."

He put his cheek against her soft hair, and he gave a deep sigh. They did not discuss the matter any further.

That afternoon when her dancing class was over, Fiona went down to Chelsea to her old flat.

She paid the rent up to due date, arranged with the landlord to give up her lease, and that until she needed it he should store her furniture for her.

While she was there the memory of Donald came to her, and she thought of how unkind she had been to him in not seeing him all this long time.

She had written to him from the Careys', saying that she had gone to friends in the country for a rest, but since her return to London she had not had the courage to seek him out.

Having packed all her personal belongings that she needed, she left the rest in charge of the landlord, and took her way slowly homewards.

There was no-one in the flat when she returned, and for once the silence seemed oppressive.

She looked round the pretty sitting-room with its huge bowls of flowers and its net curtains moving slightly in the breeze which came from the Park in at the open window.

Jim's outburst of the morning came back to her.

Why had he suddenly burst out like that, she wondered, and almost without thinking she found herself looking round his dressing-room. Was there anything there that could give her any clue?

A pile of letters lay on the writing-desk, where there was a photograph of herself in the brown leather frame.

It had been a surprise present for Jim a week ago,

and her mouth quivered in a tender smile as she remembered his pleasure at receiving a gift from her.

She glanced at the pile of letters, and then turned away quickly from them.

"I really can't read his letters," she thought, and was ashamed that the idea had even occurred to her.

She opened the drawer of his dressing-table and tidied it, putting the handkerchiefs into precise rows, laying the ties out in neat array. She opened the other drawer, then gave a little start.

Lying inside on top was a letter without an envelope.

Without meaning to read it, forced by curiosity or some instinct stronger than herself, she picked up the letter and read the concluding signature. It was: "Ann."

Somehow she had known that she would find this. Some premonition had made her search for it.

Now, when it lay within her grasp, she turned white and shaking, her hands trembling so that the letter rustled as she looked at its opening.

She read it through from beginning to end, and when she had finished she read it again. She put it back in its place, and went to her room.

She sat for a long time quite still, staring before her with eyes which saw nothing of her surroundings. The sentences she had read were seared on her brain. She felt she could never forget them, they were there before her—for ever.

"My decree will be made absolute within the next three days," was what she had read, and then, *"How I am longing to see you, my darling Jim. At last we can be married."*

"At last we can be married"—Fiona's lips moved as she repeated the words.

It had come, then—the blow had fallen. Ann was free, and her freedom meant that she—Fiona—must lose everything which meant anything in life. She had not expected it so soon.

She had known that it would happen, and subconsciously the thought was always with her. She had tried not to let it become a reality in her mind, and yet always there was a voice within her whispering:

"Be happy while you may. Enjoy yourself while you can. To-morrow all this may be gone."

What was she to do? How could she face the future without Jim? And then came the thought, bitter-sweet, that Jim would have to face the future without her.

"In three days."

Suddenly Fiona came to the decision that she could not discuss this with Jim. Whatever happened, they must leave each other without good-bye.

There are some things too intimate to be told, too intimate to be seen; some things which are too painful to be revealed.

As a person will shrink from the sight of a terrible wound, so a sensitive nature will shrink from the sight of any great emotion and from the experience of it.

"Jim mustn't tell me," Fiona thought to herself.

She went to the telephone and booked two seats at a theatre for a play they both wanted to see.

Then she went downstairs and ordered a dinner for two, choosing all Jim's favourite dishes and ordering a bottle of champagne.

"I mustn't show that I know," she said to herself. "I must pretend that I am happy. Our last night together must be gay and must be perfect."

* * *

Fiona stood in the sitting-room next morning and watched Jim walk away down the street, the sunshine on his hair as he waved gaily to her from the corner.

Then he turned it, and was hidden from view.

"Good-bye!" she whispered and hid her face in her hands.

He had gone, he had left her life, unknowingly, happy, even though the knowledge that very soon he would have to tell her about Ann was worrying him and making him restless.

For a moment Fiona was shaken by uncontrollable

tears, and then with an effort she pulled herself together. All through the previous evening she had acted and pretended as she had never done before in her life.

They had enjoyed their dinner together, had laughed over supper, and returned home while the night was still young, asking nothing more than to be alone.

They had whispered and murmured many things to each other, and Fiona felt that the night was a perfect memory which would help her through the many long and weary years to come.

The breakfast left on the table was their last meal together. When Jim returned in the evening he would find the flat empty.

Yet it was better that she should leave him like this, than that they should torture each other with hours of misery; hurting, and somehow degrading too, the perfect gladness they had enjoyed together.

And as if the gods were helping her in her plan for escape, Jim had that morning received her passport from the bank, which he had applied for in preparation for their holiday in the South of France.

"I must go abroad," Fiona had thought.

He had opened the letter in bed, and thrown her the passport, teasing her about her photograph, which, with the invariability of passport photographs, made her as plain and as unattractive as was possible.

It was then that she had thought of money. Her purse contained fifteen shillings, the remains of her last week's wages.

She would not get far on that, she thought to herself, and hating herself for asking she said:

"Can I have some money for the house-keeping? We never paid last week's bill."

Jim, before he left, had written a cheque for £25 and left it on her writing table.

"I have made it out to you," he said, "and will you pay that small account at the chemist's?"

She had promised to do so; she endorsed the cheque

now, and put it in her handbag. She packed feverishly, taking all Jim's presents with her.

She knew that even if he were angry at her sudden departure, he would hate more than anything that she should forget one of his gifts, leaving it behind to torment him with memories of her presence.

The only thing she left was her photograph, and though she felt that was unwise, she could not bear to take it away.

When she was at last ready, she realised she had only a little over three-quarters of an hour before the boat train left Victoria, and she had to call at the bank on the way.

She took a sheet of notepaper to write a line to Jim, and sat for a time looking at its whiteness, holding the pen in her hand.

She started a few words, then tore them up.

How could you write to someone you loved? What was there to say? No words could express her feelings, nothing could describe their strength. Nothing could tell him adequately how much of her heart she left behind.

How could she thank him for the only time that had meant anything in her life, the only happiness she had ever known? She could not even wish him luck in the future.

She knew that he loved her, and knew that only his honour to another woman would prevent him following her, if he knew where she was.

As quickly as she had come into his life so she must go out of it, disappearing into a world which he would never enter, a world of work, a world of sorrow.

She had had her time, had her months, she could ask nothing more.

Slowly she put the pen back in the tray. There were no words, only tears which could not be expressed.

She rang the bell for the porter, and stood silent while he took her luggage downstairs and put it on a taxi. Then she looked round the little flat in farewell.

From her dressing-table she took one pink rose from

a bunch Jim had brought home to her the night before and pinned it against her dress.

Then, dry-eyed, she walked slowly downstairs.

The Channel crossing was calm and uneventful, the train to Paris its usual swift, jolting self. Fiona had never been to Paris before. She had once been to Dieppe on a cheap day-trip from Folkestone, when she was a child.

She spoke a little French with an English accent, but nevertheless she could make herself understood.

There were two women in her compartment from Calais to Paris, both English, and after eyeing her with the usual distasteful distrust which English people travelling invariably show toward their fellow-passengers, they became quite conversational over the matter of the window.

Finally Fiona picked up courage to ask them about a cheap hotel where she could stay.

They offered her various names and addresses, and the elder of the two suggested that if she liked she could accompany them to their modest little pension, which was clean and cheap.

Fiona thanked her, but thought she would try one of the hotels they had suggested first.

An early dinner was served on the train, and Fiona thought it was perhaps wise to have a meal while she could, rather than risk trying to find one in Paris.

She enjoyed the delicious omelette, the chicken and the *bombé*—the inevitable but well-cooked meal on a French train.

She was at the far end of the second-class saloon, and could look through the glass partition at the first-class diners, who did not seem to be having a much better meal than that which the second-class enjoyed.

Through the partition she noticed immediately a dark and extremely handsome man.

He was obviously a foreigner, and Fiona hazarded a guess to herself that he had Argentine blood in him, yet he was unusually tall and broad-shouldered for a South American.

He was well dressed, if a trifle fastidiously, and she noticed that his alert glances around him seemed to take in everything and everybody. Nothing seemed to escape his attention.

He noted every passenger as they entered, scrutinising them swiftly, and yet, Fiona felt, microscopically, as though every detail about them was of interest.

When the meal was over, he lit a large cigar, smoking it with obvious enjoyment, yet never for a moment, so Fiona noticed, did he relax.

She did not know why this man interested her, but she found herself watching him as he was watching others.

A fat woman in a sable coat, massed in bad taste with expensive jewellery, entered, a pampered, over-fed Pekingese under her arm.

She dropped the dog's lead as she passed between the tables, and in a moment the dark young man had retrieved it and handed it to her with a charming smile.

She simpered her thanks, and sank down at the next table, loosening her coat and settling her dog beside her with much affection and fuss.

"I wonder who he is," Fiona thought.

Later, passing down the corridor of the first-class carriages, she looked through a window to see her dark man sitting in state. He had a rug over his knees, and an expensive-looking attaché-case was open beside him.

"He's obviously an important person," Fiona said to herself.

As she looked, she met his searching dark eyes scrutinising her, as he had scrutinized everyone else.

She blushed for having permitted herself to stare at him, and hurried away to her own carriage.

An hour later they steamed into Paris, and Fiona did not restrain the thrill of the thought that here she was at last, in the City of which she had heard so much.

She stood for a long time forlornly trying to get a porter. When finally one came, she managed to make him understand that she wanted a taxi to drive her to the Hôtel Voltaire.

She had chosen at random to go to this hotel, out of the list the ladies in the train had given her.

She arrived at the hotel, with its unpretentious entrance and tired concierge at his tiny desk. It seemed a poor place, but her bedroom, when she was taken to it, was scrupulously clean.

She pulled off her hat, took off her coat and her shoes, and then suddenly she could bear it no longer.

Sobbing Jim's name, she buried her face in the pillow and cried bitterly.

*　　*　　*

After four days of wandering around, Fiona began to realise that to find a job was not going to be as easy as she had thought.

It was nearly August, and most of the dancing places were closing for the season, their staffs drifting away to Monte Carlo, Cannes, Biarritz, ready to follow their patrons wherever they went.

She had sought a job as a mannequin at a famous costumier's not far from the Place Vendôme, to find her request greeted with jovial laughter.

"We are turning them away, *ma chérie*," the fat proprietor had informed her, "turning them away! However, come back in September, and I will see what I can do for you."

Disheartened, Fiona walked slowly down the street. The heat from the pavements seemed to rise into her feet as she walked, contracting her patent-leather shoes.

She longed for a cool drink of lemonade at a restaurant, but felt that one-franc-fifty would be extravagant.

It would be needed for solid food soon, she told herself, and dismissed the temptation to sit outside a café where the bright striped awning offered shady protection.

She knew if she approached one of the inviting-looking wicker-chairs she would have to order something.

Instead, greatly daring, she crossed the Place Vendôme and entered the cool great hall of the famous Ritz hotel.

The reading-room lay to her left, with papers of every nationality spread out on the marble-topped table, while large cushioned arm-chairs invited the reader, and those in need of forty-winks.

Conscious that though she had no business within its portals, her smart clothes were a passport which would ensure her entering without question.

Fiona walked slowly through the pillared entrance, passed two commissionaires, and taking the English *Times* from the table sat down in an arm-chair.

She had not been there long when she heard some one enter, and glancing up saw the back of a man who was idly turning over the pages of a paper.

He was vaguely familiar, and as Fiona wondered where she had seen him before, he turned, and she recognised the dark man she had seen on her train journey.

Their eyes met, and instantaneously he recognised her, for he gave her an almost imperceptible smile and made a slight movement, as though he would have bowed, and then corrected himself.

Fiona went on looking at her paper, at the same time watching him with interest. He was well dressed, but—as she had noticed before—a shade too fastidiously.

After a moment of looking at the papers, he put them down and walked past Fiona to a writing-table which lay beyond her. It was facing in her direction, and Fiona had the uneasy feeling that while he wrote he was at the same time scrutinising her.

Glad of the rest, she was determined that however critically he regarded her she would not be driven away.

Yet, feminine-like she could not refrain from powdering her nose, looking in her minute mirror to see if she were tidy.

In a few minutes, the man rose and walked past her

again, and as he passed he dropped the letters which he carried, at her feet.

It was such a transparent trick to invite her conversation that Fiona was amused at the obviousness of it, especially as, with a *"Pardon, Madame,"* he bent slowly to collect his scattered mail.

"It is so clumsy of me—I am sorry," the stranger added, speaking in English.

"That's all right," Fiona answered coldly.

With as much dignity as she could, she returned to the perusal of her paper.

However, the dark man was not to be so easily put off.

"I am sure you would forgive my asking you," he said, "but could you tell me in what street Claridge's Hotel is, in London?"

As his letters were already addressed and stamped, Fiona did not think this was a very ingenious question, even on the spur of the moment.

However, it was not worth while being rude; so she told him "Brook Street," and went back to her paper.

There was a silence after her remark, and quite without thinking she looked up to see why he had not moved. He was smiling at her, and as their eyes met she could not help smiling in return, at the very impertinence of him.

"Don't be cross," he said, as swiftly she tried to check her smile. "I do so want to talk to you."

Before she could say anything he sat down in the next chair.

"Do talk to me," he said. "I saw you on the train, and I wondered then who you were and where you were going."

There was no doubt his manner was very charming and somehow after four days of loneliness it was good to hear someone talking English again, even with an accent—someone talking to her as an equal, and not as the scornful proprietor of some job.

Almost before she realised it, Fiona was laughing

over the train journey, and a moment later she had told him of her search for a job.

"You are looking for a job?" he echoed incredulously. "But that is extraordinary! You look—what shall I say?—very rich!"

Fiona laughed and shook her head.

"Relics of prosperous days," she said, "if you mean my clothes. But I have simply got to find something to do within the next forty-eight hours."

"Come and lunch with me," he begged.

'Why shouldn't I?' thought Fiona. 'After all, I'm hungry, and I shall save money. He seems quite nice, and not dangerous so far.'

After a moment's hesitation she accepted.

"Good!" he said. "Where shall we lunch?"

Fiona laughed, and replied: "Why ask me? I don't know good places in Paris."

"Then we'll lunch here," he said, "because I want to talk to you. By the way, my name is Rémon—and yours?"

"Fiona," she replied, rather glad that his lead of not giving her his surname had saved her giving hers.

They went in to lunch, choosing a table in the big window which looked onto the tiny garden.

She enjoyed her lunch and found her companion on acquaintance to be charming and intelligent.

He knew London well, but he assured her he was happier in France, where he had made his home.

"But I am a traveller," he added. "I am here, there and everywhere. Yet France is now—how shall I put it in your words?—my home town."

"Rather a large one," she suggested, but he shook his head.

"The people are the same," he said, "from the north to the south, though they pretend they are different. I find them always the same. Happy, thrifty, gay and pleased to see one—I hope."

He added the last words with a curious emphasis, and Fiona had the impression that he was laughing a little at himself, at a joke in which she could not participate.

Encouraged by his friendliness, she consulted him quite seriously as to what she should do.

"I don't know why I should bother you with my affairs," she said, "but I am rather worried at the moment. I can't go on like this, I must get a job as quickly as possible before my last few pounds have dwindled away.

"What do you think it is possible to get at this time of year? I see now that I couldn't have come to Paris at a worse time in search of work."

"It is always difficult, the type of work you require—respectable work," he answered. "French people are not keen on letting strangers take money from them. They like the strangers to do the giving."

"You are not very encouraging," Fiona sighed.

"My dear," he said, "I'm speaking the truth. You had better go back to England while you can afford the fare."

"I can't do that," Fiona said quickly.

Interestedly he watched the expression on her face as she answered him. Then he said,

"You mean you can't go back?"

Fiona answered him quite frankly.

"I mean there are circumstances which make it imperative that I shouldn't," she said, a little abruptly.

But she was trying to keep the longing out of her voice, the longing for England, for dear old London, and above all the longing which had become a never-ceasing ache for Jim.

"I wonder," Rémon said, contemplative, looking at her.

Then, as Fiona raised her eyes to his questioningly, he continued,

"I wonder if you could do a job for me?"

"I'd love to," Fiona said. "Is it something I could do?"

"Something you could do," Rémon replied, "but whether you would do it is another matter. But I would be prepared to pay you eight thousand francs if you would do it."

97

"Nearly a hundred pounds!" Fiona exclaimed, and then quickly to her mind came the sudden suspicion:

Why should a man pay a woman a lot of money, except for one reason? Yet even as the suspicion came into her thoughts, he seemed to read it, and shook his head kindly.

"No, my dear," he said, "not that. You are very pretty—but not that."

Fiona put her hands under her chin and regarded him intently.

"Tell me," she said. "If it is possible, I will do it."

He looked at her long and searchingly with those strange, dark eyes, which, Fiona had noticed the first time she saw them, seemed to scrutinise every detail of the person they regarded.

"Can I trust you?" he said. "Can I honestly rely on you?"

Fiona nodded her head.

"You can," she said, "I promise you."

Rémon looked round the room. They had sat a long time over luncheon, and the tables near them had been emptying rapidly.

There was no one within earshot of them. As he looked round, with that swift, penetrating glance, Fiona thought to herself,

"I know what he's like—he's like a panther, good-looking, sleek, and yet savage under that handsome exterior. What can he want of me? What can I do?"

At the same time, there was something about the man she liked, some responsive chord in herself which made her feel that somehow she could trust him.

Fiona had met so many men in her life, men who had always grasped at her, tried to take something from her.

She had a mental nightmare of them striving to get at her with clutching hands, of requiring her always physically, of trying to snatch at her and her attractions.

Yet with Rémon she had the feeling that his brain, cool, calculating to the 'nth degree, had summed her up and found her desirable in an utterly different way.

She knew now that there would be no affection between them, but somehow there was an understanding.

And so, as he turned from scrutinising the room and the adjacent tables, she held out her hand.

"I will trust you if you will trust me," she said.

Rémon took it for a moment.

"That's just what I'm going to do," he said.

CHAPTER FIVE

Mrs. Angus Vansittart was humming to herself un-tunefully a little melody, as she smeared her face with cream.

The mirrors showed her hair too stiffly waved, the roots having a darkness which repeated applications of brightening dyes could not completely eradicate.

They showed a flabby skin which no amount of cosmetics could entirely conceal.

They showed a weak, sensuous mouth, which, even as it hummed, greedily demanded more of life than it was ever likely to obtain.

Mrs. Vansittart's maid hovered by the safe, waiting for her mistress to finish spreading powder heavily over her chin and throat, before she asked,

"Will you wear the emeralds or your pearls to-night, Madame?"

Mrs. Vansittart considered this momentous question with becoming gravity.

"The emeralds—no, the pearls—no: it had better be the emeralds. I think Mr. Rémon admires the emeralds most, don't you, Parker?"

"He certainly admired them the last time you wore them, Madame," said Parker, "do you remember—with the silver dress?"

Mrs. Vansittart nodded.

"Yes, you are right, Parker, but I think they will go just as nicely with my new white Chanel. Yes, Parker, I will wear the emeralds."

Parker brought out the cases and opened them, to reveal the large gems flashing from beds of white velvet, surrounded by glittering diamonds.

"Now finish my hair," Mrs. Vansittart commanded.

Obediently Parker picked up the tortoiseshell comb. Outwardly humble and subservient, she was saying to herself,

"The old fool! I wish she'd hurry up. I shall keep André waiting again. I wonder if he will be angry tonight. It is all this silly old woman's fault, for not making up her mind what she's going to wear till the last moment!"

She gave a curl under her fingers a sharp tweak, so that Mrs. Vansittart gave a shrill cry.

"Do be careful, Parker—please! That hurt me."

"It looks lovely now, Madame," Parker replied.

She had learnt that flattery was the only thing that could get her mistress dressed in anything like a reasonable space of time.

Mrs. Vansittart made a little *moue* of pleasure at herself in the glass.

"I must say this new hairdresser does know his job, Parker. My hair is looking better than it ever has before."

"And you too, Madame—if I may venture to say so," Parker added, "but perhaps it is because you are happier."

Mrs. Vansittart stood up, and made an almost kittenish skip.

"Perhaps you are right, Parker—perhaps it is happiness," she said. "And now my dress."

Her corsetted figure was eased gently and carefully into the new dress. It fitted very tightly, but it gave Mrs. Vansittart some semblance of having a modern straight, flat figure.

She hummed with pleasure at her reflection in the glass, then, clasping over her whitened arms her many emerald bracelets, she allowed Parker to put round her neck the emerald and diamond necklace.

The whole effect was rather gaudy, but Mrs. Vansittart was well pleased.

Just then the telephone bell rang.

"See who it is, Parker," she said.

"Yes, Monsieur—yes," Parker answered, "yes—Madame is wearing her emeralds. Yes—I am sure those would go beautifully, thank you very much, Monsieur. Madame is nearly ready."

"Monsieur Rémon, Madame," Parker repeated, "and he says he hopes you will wear your emeralds, as he is bringing you green orchids."

"Now, isn't that lucky, Parker!" Mrs. Vansittart said. "It's just luck that we had decided already to wear the emeralds!"

Monsieur Rémon was only kept waiting a meagre quarter of an hour in the ornately decorated sitting-room, before his hostess entered and greeted him, smiling, glittering, and smelling like an Oriental bazaar.

"*Chèrie!*" Rémon said.

He took her hand in his and pressed his lips to it.

"I have ordered you dinner at the *Bal Masque*," he continued, after several minutes of effusive compliments and equally effusive simperings from Mrs. Vansittart.

"Heaven!" she said girlishly. "Let us go."

"One thing I want to ask you," he said urgently. "Let us have supper here to-night. I want to talk to you alone. I never see you except surrounded by hundreds of your admirers."

"What a flatterer, you are, Rémon!" she replied. "But if you would really like to have supper here . . ."

She seemed a little doubtful.

"My husband—" she hesitated.

"He is away, and he will never know," Rémon said. "Let us be happy for once—please!"

His handsome face pleading, would have melted a far more adamant heart than that of Mrs. Vansittart, which was fluttering with delightful apprehensions.

"All right," she said at last.

She took up the telephone and ordered champagne and caviare to be awaiting her return.

They went downstairs to where Mrs. Vansittart's car —a huge, luxurious Hispano-Suiza—awaited them. Under the warm sable rug Rémon held her hand, as they sped towards the music and lights of the *Bal Masque*.

Four hours later the same car glided silently back with them to the door of the apartment. Taking a gold key from her bag. Rémon opened the door and let Mrs. Vansittart precede him.

The sitting-room, with its low, shaded lights, its embroidered cushions, and napkin-wrapped bottle of champagne, looked like a scene from some super-Hollywood film.

Mrs. Vansittart, who had already dined well, felt her senses reeling a little with excitement and pleasurable anticipation. She felt deliciously naughty, provocative, and in love.

As he drew the ermine wrap from her shoulders, Rémon just touched her shoulder with his lips. A girlish giggle told him that his action had not passed unnoticed.

"Open the champagne," she said.

She helped him with a liberal hand from the large pot of caviare.

Rémon raised his glass to his lips, and murmured in French an audacious toast.

Mrs. Vansittart, who only understood two words— "eyes" and "beautiful"—giggled, and hoped it was as improper as his eyes seemed to suggest.

She had a feeling that Rémon was getting more than a little fond of her.

She rose and moved, rather unsteadily on her too high heels, towards the over-befrilled sofa with its soft cushions and imitation tapestry back.

"Come and talk to me," she said, with a glance which she believed to be eloquent in its appeal.

Rémon put down his glass and moved gracefully across to join her.

"Sadie," he said, "I have something to tell you."

At the husky depths of his voice Sadie shivered, pleasantly apprehensive.

"Sadie!" Rémon repeated.

He held out his arms, and she threw herself into them, abandoning herself to an ecstasy which quite frightened her with its intensity.

A few minutes later, Rémon took the heavy jewelled necklace from around her neck.

"It gets in my way," he said, and she gave an eager laugh.

Ten minutes after that, Sadie, dishevelled, her curls, which had started the evening so crisp and neat from the hairdresser's hand's, tumbled in golden disarray against Rémon's dark shoulder.

On the floor, the emerald bracelets glittered on the thick carpet, thrown there disdainfully under the impulse of love by a woman who had worked her husband nearly to death to procure them for her.

Almost noiselessly the handle of the door turned, and suddenly it was wide open, and in the doorway, dressed severely in black, stood another woman.

Sadie Vansittart gave a shrill scream, and struggled to regain her feet from her ignominious position.

"Who is it?" she said. "What do you want?"

But her voice was shrill, and her efforts to stand while she adjusted her shoulder-straps and tidied her hair were not only undignified but ludicrous.

It was then she heard Rémon say:

"*Mon Dieu!* My wife!"

The woman in the doorway came further into the room. She was very white in the face, as if the shock had been tremendous.

"So this is how you behave!" she said to the apparently terrified Rémon. "And who is this woman?"

Sadie was staring at Rémon.

"Your wife?" she said. "I had no idea—"

But she was cut short by the woman in black.

"Of course you had no idea," she said, "nor had I. But I gathered from his letters that he was in love with somebody else. Very well, then. If he loves you as much as that, you can have him. I'm through with him. I shall file my divorce to-morrow, and cite you as co-respondent."

"Co-respondent!" Sadie gave a shrill scream of horror. "But you can't prove anything against me—I have done nothing!"

"Oh no?" *Madame* gave her a searching look. "What about being alone with my husband at this hour of the morning? Perhaps you, too have a husband. Would you care for him to behave like this?"

"My husband!" Sadie put her hand to her head, and turned to the still speechless Rémon. "You can't let your wife behave like this—do you hear? My husband will know of it—he will hear—he will divorce me too. Oh, my God! Can't you stop this mad woman?"

"You should think of all that before you play about with other people's husbands," *Madame* Rémon said severely. "I have nothing more to say on the matter. Rémon, you will hear from my solicitors in the morning —and you also, Madam, in due course."

She walked towards the door, but she had not reached it before Sadie flung herself before her.

"Stop!" she said. "Stop her, Rémon! You must listen to me. I swear to you your husband means nothing to me. Take him back—and I promise you that I will have nothing to do with him again. Rémon, do please ask her —please! Rémon!

"You don't know what is at stake—my whole life— I cannot let my husband know of this."

Madame appeared to hesitate.

"I do not know that I want him back," she said. "You have taken his love from me, and you have given him expensive tastes. Look at this room—that food—"

She intimated with a vague hand the champagne and caviare,

"We are poor people, we cannot afford to live like that. You lead him astray, and you steal him. Perhaps you had better keep him. I cannot afford him."

Again she moved towards the door, but Sadie held her back.

"Don't go," she said. "I will give you money, I will

give you anything, only don't involve me in this scandal."

Madame looked at her coldly. In her dark clothes, compared with the other woman's dishevelled finery, she was far the more imposing figure.

"Very well," she said, "I will take him back. But you must give me one hundred thousands francs, and you must promise not to communicate with him again."

"A hundred thousand francs!" Sadie looked aghast for a moment.

"If not—you keep him."

With tears in her voice, Sadie replied,

"No—no, I will give it you—I will give it to you now. Where is my cheque-book?"

Mrs. Vansittart searched feverishly in the drawers of the Louis Quinze writing-table, scattering papers in all directions as her nervous hands sought here and there.

At last the book was found, and taking up the gold pen from the china inkstand, with trembling fingers she wrote a cheque for the desired amount. She handed it to the woman, who scrutinised it, and then said:

"If this is stopped, you will know what to expect."

Without another word, the two left the flat, and only as the door closed behind them did Sadie Vansittart burst into hysterical sobs, from which it took her some minutes to recover.

In fact, it was nearly half an hour later before she discovered that her emeralds were missing.

Although she thought for a long time, she could find no possible way in which she could ever recover them.

*   *   *

Fiona and Rémon walked out of the bank with smiling faces into a morning of brilliant sunshine, piercing the haze over Paris, foretelling great heat later in the day.

It was very early, and although inside the bank all was briskness and precision, the streets were comparatively empty.

In Rémon's breast-pocket was a packet which crackled as he moved.

He could not help letting his hand move involuntarily now and again to touch it, and each time he did so his eyes met Fiona's in a quaint smile.

They walked together some way from the bank before either of them spoke, and eventually found themselves outside a small café.

The waiter was busily cleaning the interior, but the bright-rimmed little tables on the pavement were already polished and dusted, awaiting customers.

Rémon ordered two coffees and *brioches,* and as the waiter departed he held out his hand to Fiona.

"Well done, comrade," he said.

Fiona laughed.

"I've never been so frightened in my life."

"You were splendid," he replied, "and now you are packed?"

"Yes," Fiona answered, "but where am I to go?"

Rémon wrinkled his forehead.

"Where would you like to go?" he asked. "I think it is better for us both to leave this charming city for a little while. I personally am taking an aeroplane to Amsterdam, where they are interested in and not superstitious about—shall we say?—green stones."

Fiona shrugged her shoulders.

"I don't mind," she confessed.

"Then I should try Monte Carlo," Rémon said. "There is always something doing there. All the world and his wife will be down there within a week or so, and you might easily find a job.

"There are plenty," he continued, with a meaning smile; "not perhaps the ones you would like, but nevertheless jobs. However, my little comrade, I can only wish you good luck and hope you will find something.

"And now, if you have finished your coffee, shall we take a taxi, because I have some notes to convey to you, and I do not think it is wise to give them to you here."

Laughing at his serious way of putting things, Fiona agreed. In the taxi, he handed her eight thousand francs.

Then, tapping on the window, he told the driver to drop him on the corner of the Place de la Concorde, leaving Fiona to proceed alone to her hotel.

As the taxi stopped, he took her hand in his and kissed it very gently.

"You are brave and very sweet," he said. *"Bon voyage,* and take care of yourself. We shall meet again some day."

"Good-bye," Fiona replied.

A moment later he was walking away from her with his easy graceful gait, and though she watched him through the window in the back of the taxi, he did not look round.

An hour later Fiona was on board the train for Monte Carlo.

She had decided to travel by day, for apart from the fact that Rémon thought it wiser that they should both leave Paris as soon as possible, she also did not wish to waste an extra two hundred francs on sleeping accommodation.

All through the long day that followed she sat watching the country, or trying to read, but her mind was living over and over again the events of the night before.

How easy last night seemed now, the job smoothly and competently executed! And yet—"blackmail" was a terrifying word, a word which conjured up the thought of long years in prison.

"I'm a crook," Fiona thought to herself. "How awful —and yet how exciting! All this is rather like living in a detective novel. But for me there is no happy ending."

The thought of Jim brought tears to her eyes. She still could not think of him without her heart aching intolerably and the longing for him being an intense agony.

She wondered what he was doing now, as she had wondered practically every moment since she had left him.

What had he said, what had he felt, when he returned to that empty flat to find her gone? Gone, without even leaving a note behind.

She felt somehow he would understand this lapse on her part. Jim, who knew her so well, would know it was not callousness or thoughtlessness—he had teased her so often about her inability to express herself really forcibly.

She remembered how he used to tease her and make her say she loved him.

"I love you," Fiona would say obediently, her eyes, raised to his, leaving him no doubt that she spoke the truth.

"But how much?" he would ask. "Tell me how much."

And Fiona would shake her head, refusing to be drawn into an argument, and Jim would tease her unmercifully about what he called her dumbness.

He himself would tell her eloquently how lovely she was, how much she meant to him, how deeply happy he was in her presence, and she would long to be able to answer him in return.

Yet she had no words to express her appreciation of being with him.

To tell him that the mere fact of his presence near her seemed like a magnet which drew all her being quiveringly to him, so that she felt she was part of him, utterly and completely.

She could only say in words, "I love you, Jim," and leave it at that.

It was night when her train reached Monte Carlo. It ran along the Corniche road, passing through Cannes and Nice, ablaze with lights, and travelling in the purple dusk through romantically dark places.

It was only when they drew up at the tiny station of Monte Carlo that Fiona realised she had no idea what hotel to go to.

Secure in the knowledge that her bag contained over eight thousand francs, she was not as anxious as she had been on arriving in Paris, but nevertheless she was determined that this money should last her as long as possible.

She did not wish to have to take whatever chance fate might bring to provide her with bread-and-butter.

In her halting French, she asked the man at the gate if he could recommend her to a good, cheap hotel.

He looked at her quickly, and then reassured, perhaps, by her quiet air and pale face after the tiring journey, he answered:

"There is a nice little hotel, the Rigi, not far from the Winter Casino."

Thanking him, Fiona trudged up the hill, accompanied by an out-porter with her luggage. The hotel was small, respectable and unpretentious.

For a few francs a day, Fiona could have a room, or for double the amount she could be *en pension*.

She agreed to try the latter terms for a day or so, until she found her feet in this new and strange life.

She was far too weary to explore Monte Carlo that night, and unpacking a few of her things she got into bed, and slept a sound, dreamless sleep.

When she awoke the sun was streaming in through her shutters, making a variegated pattern in the room.

"Like prison bars," Fiona said to herself.

A little shiver of fear made her jump out of bed and fling them wide open.

The sight that met her eyes made her gasp. Never had she seen a sky so intensely blue.

Away below her she could catch a glimpse of the famous beach, the sugar-pink buildings of the new hotels, and a large white edifice like a wedding-cake, with terraces below, which she guessed to be the Casino.

It was very hot, but what breeze there was swept in at Fiona's window, for she was high above the roofs below.

Fiona did not take long to dress, and she spent the morning exploring the town, the famous terraces, and watching people disport themselves in the swimming pool or oiling their backs, as they lay around, almost sizzling in the sun, on orange mattresses.

Fiona realised that she had better buy herself a bathing-dress.

But she was wise enough to avoid the expensive shops, and after lunch at her hotel she wandered up the narrow streets of the town, and managed to purchase for only a few francs, in an unfrequented thoroughfare, a smart white woollen suit.

She bathed that afternoon, but felt a little shy amongst the eager throngs of people who all seemed to know each other intimately.

After her bathe, she sat in a corner of the swimming-pool and watched the people for a little while. Soon she noticed that another person was doing the same thing.

He was an old man of perhaps seventy, once good-looking, but now he seemed ill, for he leant back in his chair with an exhausted air.

His grey hair was brushed back from a broad forehead and a moustache hid a clever but kindly mouth.

His eyes, Fiona thought as she watched him, were rather pathetic.

He seemed to want to join the young people who splashed and shouted and giggled around him, but was obviously not well enough to do so, and besides he seemed to be very much alone.

As if he felt her scrutiny, after a while he glanced up and met her eyes, and before Fiona could look away gave her a little smile, as though he recognised that she too was alone.

Fiona got up and walked slowly homewards. On her way, she called at the Casino, and producing her passport took out a ticket to the rooms.

She felt this was a terrible extravagance, but at the same time it did not seem natural that she should be in Monte Carlo and not go to the Casino in the evening.

"After all," she argued with her conscience, which told her she was being extravagant, "I am not likely to get a job by sitting here indoors and looking at the wallpaper. I must get out and about, meet people, and perhaps I shall find something."

While she was at the Casino she enquired whether they wanted any dancers on the roof.

They had plenty of girls, they informed her, but at

the same time were willing to take her address in case a chance presented itself.

The man who interviewed her was quite pleasant, and Fiona was able to obtain from him information as to dancing places in the town, where she might be likely to find a job.

"If you wait long enough," she was told, "there is sure to be a vacancy. Heaps of girls come down here at the beginning of the season. Some are fortunate—they find better and more lucrative posts."

He winked as he spoke, and Fiona knew exactly to what type of post he referred.

"Others are less fortunate—they get ill, and the doctor sends them away."

There was no doubt of his meaning this time either.

"But whichever it is, good luck or bad, it leaves room for another to step into their shoes."

Fiona thanked him, and, going back to her hotel, unpacked her things and chose a dress suitable for the evening. She could not be too grateful that Jim had insisted on providing her with a beautiful wardrobe.

The dress she decided on was white, very simply made, but betraying a great dressmaker in every line which fell in becoming folds about her slim figure.

She had dinner downstairs in the *pension* dining-room and afterwards placing a velvet wrap over her shoulders she walked slowly down the dark road.

The Summer Casino was ablaze with flood-lights. In front of it, in the sea, was an island, built as a stage, on which a cabaret entertainment amused the hundreds of diners who sat on the long terraces being served with food, as they listened to the massed bands.

She was early, Fiona realised. No one in fashionable Monte Carlo seemed to dine until nearly ten o'clock.

A little self-conscious, she wandered into the gambling rooms, where the croupiers sat alert at the tables, waiting for the first fly to enter into the spider's parlour.

Huge windows opened on to the terrace, and she sat on the cushioned seat before one of these and watched the people below.

Sitting alone at a table in a corner, Fiona saw the old man she had noticed in the afternoon by the swimming-pool.

She watched him eat frugally, and a little fastidiously, the food before him, sipping at a glass of Vichy water—a strange contrast to the bottles of champagne which were being drunk at every table around him.

People, as they finished dinner, began to drift in to "the tables," to the roof garden, to the lounge hall, where they sat watching each other, increasingly interested and curious about their fellow-creatures.

The roulette tables in the rooms began to fill up. The cry of the croupiers, *"Faites vos jeux,"* the click of the roulette balls and the numbers called out, mixed in a very strange music with the moan of the waves below.

As the terrace emptied and the room filled, Fiona felt she would like to go outside.

She wished somehow to seek the open air. She could not yet begin to interest herself in "the tables," of which she had heard so much.

She wandered on to the now almost deserted terrace, and stood for a while watching lights gleam on the sea below, turning the ever-moving water into a kaleidoscope of lovely colours, purple, green and crimson, against the rocks.

As she stood lost in her thoughts, she was brought back to reality by a voice which said:

"You seem lonely, too. May I speak to you?"

* * *

It was two weeks before Fiona heard the whole story of Andrew Uckfield's life, and by then they were firm friends.

A North Country man, he had been brought up to work, as his father had before him, in the cotton mills which, after he had taken over the business, increased in size until they employed thousands of hands.

He delighted to work, and delighted in knowing that he commanded, as it were, this army of workers; that

113

the great machines worked because he willed it; that he could purchase their energy; to him that was as romantic as any story ever written.

Then one day he married his first cousin, the result of the determined matchmaking of his sisters. The marriage was dull, conventional and uninspired.

They neither of them were in love with the other, it was a marriage of convenience, and as such it remained.

She ran his house successfully, and took her place as the wife of one of the richest men in the district, but she made no attempt to understand or appreciate her husband or his qualities.

He was equally to blame—he thought her a handsome woman, and he gave her any money she asked for, but how she spent her days was a subject which never interested him and on which he never thought to enquire.

He had hoped for a son, or indeed offspring of either sex, but whether it was the fact of relationship or whether nature itself rebelled at such an unintimate match, they had no child.

The cotton strike after the War, and later the slump in trade, seriously affected his business. One of his factories was forced to close down, another continued with only half the original working staff.

Quite suddenly Andrew Uckfield found himself with little to do. He had always been advancing, improving, altering.

All his life his vast profits had gone back into the business, had been used for progress, re-invested to make his industry more valuable than it was.

Now he found there was no need to do this—in fact, it was impossible. He could not progress further, he could only sit back and save what was left to him.

He was still a very rich man, for he had spent only a tenth of what he earned. But that was not the fact that worried him.

The thing which startled him to a consciousness of himself was that he suddenly discovered he was old.

It seemed to him only yesterday that he was a young

114

boy, entering his father's factory, full of power and enthusiasm, inspired with ideas for the future, ideas for himself and for his people, most of which he later had the chance of carrying out. Now most of his life work had been swept away.

While he was still reviewing this amazing turn of affairs he was taken seriously ill. Pleurisy affected one of his lungs—it was the old story of weakness from being continually in a confined atmosphere.

From taking too little exercise and breathing too little fresh air, or working too hard and too long without any break or recreation.

The doctor, somewhat dubiously, ordered him rest, quiet, and a trip abroad, and to his surprise Andrew Uckfield agreed.

Then, after a few private words with his patient, the doctor added that he was to go alone. Mrs. Uckfield was surprised, shocked, and at first incredulous.

"A wife's place is by her husband's side," she repeated over and over again.

But the doctor was firm, and so was Andrew himself.

"Complete change from his usual life," the doctor said, and Andrew nodded his head.

The next few days alarmed his wife far more than his previous illness. He was like a schoolboy.

He took very little clothes with him, and she had a vague suspicion that he intended to buy others—and not from the good local tailor who had supplied Andrew for fifty years with the serviceable homespun which he continually wore.

A month later he wrote home that he would not be returning for some time. Two months later he repeated almost word for word the terms of his first letter.

Mrs. Uckfieid wrote and pleaded that she might join him, but did not receive an answer for some time, and then his reply was one word—"impossible."

She had postcards from him at irregular intervals, announcing that he was alive and well. He seemed to be travelling, moving all over Europe.

Postcards would come from this capital and that,

from a gay watering-place in Spain or a small village in the Alps. Finally he had written to her from Monte Carlo.

His first draught of life had made him feel oddly self-conscious and a little frightened. He had very nearly returned home, to the comfortable security of things he understood.

And then his long years of reserve and concentration stood him in good stead.

He was not afraid of loneliness, and he had always enjoyed watching people and striving to grasp their psychology, without becoming part of their lives.

He noticed Fiona at once. It was difficult for people not to notice her fair hair, the way she carried her head, and her lovely complexion, which was yet a little too pale to be absolutely healthy.

When he spoke to her, he was frightened of a rebuff. In all his peregrinations he had not spoken to very many women.

Men and boys of a certain class were generally pleased to talk to him. They sensed an interest, and human nature is seldom averse to a confessor.

With women he was more nervous. He had met so few, and understood them so little.

Andrew Uckfield, after a week of Fiona's company, realised what he had missed in life.

Intensely a masculine man, he would have loved many women had not all his virility, all his masculinity, been entirely absorbed in the fire of his work.

Had any woman chosen to secure his heart, he would have made her a perfect husband. He liked fragility, he liked the feeling of power as he had enjoyed it in his factory.

But at the same time, he would have been content, with the strong man's weakness, to worship at the feet of a woman he loved.

In Fiona he found a materialisation of his conception of what a woman should be. He adored her pretty ways, her fragile appearance, the instinctive manner in which she looked to a man to take care of her in small things.

He loved her whole vague, un-matter-of-fact manner of drifting life, hoping for chance to save her from starvation.

That was how a woman should be, he considered—he detested women who could look after themselves, arranging their lives cleverly and competently, and were prepared to equal a man at his own job, or even beat him at his own game.

It was little by little that he drew Fiona's story from her, and it was still more slowly that she gathered the story of his life from him.

When after three weeks' acquaintanceship they knew a good deal about each other, they felt mutual admiration and an affection which had grown from association.

It was one night when they were dining together at the Casino, on the same terrace where they had met, that Andrew Uckfield finally unburdened himself.

Fiona was looking very lovely as she faced him across the narrow table. She wore a dark green dress, and against it a long spray of purple orchids which Andrew had given her that evening.

Her fair hair was curled like a halo about her head, framing her face, which already was rounder and less peaked from the good food and the sunshine.

Her eyes, wide and grave, fixed themselves on his as he talked, her dark lashes curling upwards towards the narrow eyebrows.

Very lovely and very young—yet Andrew began his story and finished it, with the determination of a man who, having decided on some course in life, has always gone through with it.

"Fiona," he said gravely, "I have not very long to live.—No, no, don't speak. I will say all I have to say, my dear. Give me your answer afterwards. I am an old man, and I have perhaps worked too hard.

"Other men may live to be much older than I am, but at the same time, like an engine which will go on no longer, I think I shall soon have finished my part in this world.

"I have had very little fun in my life, as I think I

117

have told you before. I never knew how to play, and I never learned how to until now, in my old age, and now playtime must consist of sitting in the sun and watching other people.

"I have met few women in my life. I have no memories tied up in pink ribbon, and put away in a drawer, no faded roses of sentiment, no dance programmes hidden away with a kid glove, which I could kiss in happy remembrance.

"There is only one memory stored in my heart, Fiona, and that is of you this last week and the times we have spent together.

"Those memories are my happiest and my most vivid. My dear, I'm an old man and an ill man—will you make the last years of my life happy?

"I say years optimistically, it may be it will only be months.

"Will you come and live with me and go with me wherever I go? I don't mean 'live' in the way the world always thinks of it. I wish I did.

"Were I twenty years younger, things might be different. Even then I should be too old for you, yet at the same time I should do my best to make you love me.

"I can't ask you to share my life as a man, Fiona, but I can ask you to share it as a friend. I don't want to go on seeing you in scraps as we do now.

"I want you with me because I love you, and that the love which I wish to give you can only be the admiration and affection of an old man, is to me my greatest tragedy.

"I would give up all the world if I could be young enough for us to be 'in love.' But as it is I can offer you my love in the only way possible for me.

"Let me give you things, Fiona, let me try and make you happy, and if you will allow me this, you will make me the happiest man in the world. Will you, my dear?— Will you say 'yes'?"

As Andrew finished, Fiona put out both her hands impulsively across the table, and took his.

"Oh, my dear," she said, and there were tears in her eyes, "of course the answer is 'yes'!"

Then began for Fiona a time of peace and luxury, of enjoyment and happiness.

Andrew Uckfield was kindness and consideration itself to her. He loved her in an unselfish way which was unusual and in itself a lesson to Fiona.

It was impossible not to be sweet and nice to him in return.

He thought of her in every possible way. He anticipated her every wish, and she became genuinely fond of him.

She moved from her small hotel to the new luxurious one on the beach, where Andrew had a large suite of rooms. Her bedroom was enormous, big enough to hold the whole of her tiny Chelsea flat.

Andrew hired a car, and they spent many hours exploring the country around, driving over to the places along the coast, to Nice, Villefranche, Cannes, or going up to Mont Agel for lunch.

He insisted on buying her the most exquisite clothes from all the best French shops, and Fiona, accustomed to pay a few pounds for her clothes, was horrified at the prices charged for a mere wisp of white chiffon, or for an original beach dress, backless and hardly reaching below the knees.

But Andrew laughed at her scruples, and had she not restrained him, would have bought her the whole shop.

"I've save up all my life for this," he said, "and I'm not going to stop now."

He gave her a small but perfectly set diamond brooch and a bracelet, and in the depths of his generosity promised her that he was going to leave her some money in his will.

"What will your wife say?" Fiona asked anxiously.

"My dear," Andrew said, "had I had a daughter she might have been your age. You are dearer to me than any daughter could possible be. If I can't make your life happier, then I shall indeed have worked in vain."

When she had been with him for nearly a month,

Fiona, in a burst of confidence, told Andrew about the eight thousand francs she had earned in Paris.

Until then she had kept it as a secret, ashamed in her heart of her share in the matter, yet glad that the "framing" of Mrs. Vansittart had rendered it possible for her to meet Andrew Uckfield.

Andrew chuckled when she first told him the story, and then was horrified that she should have had to do such a thing.

"You must never do anything like that again," he said; "promise me, my dear. It might mean prison for you, and that's a thing I can't bear even to imagine. It's bad money—money that comes by dishonest means always is. Let us give it away, Fiona, darling, and I will refund you a thousand times."

Touched by the thought, while laughing at his superstition, Fiona agreed. There was a little chapel high up on the hill above Monte Carlo.

It was very poor, and the images which the peasants The gilt had worn from the branched candlesticks, and shabby.

The altar held its fresh field flowers in cracked vases. The gilt had worn from the branches candlesticks, and the altar-cloth was torn and stained.

Its little congregation were devout Catholics; at the same time, their purses were strained to their utmost to provide food for themselves and their families.

Fiona had come across this church on one of her peregrinations with Andrew in the car.

They had stopped, and were struck by its quiet charm, and the following Sunday, more out of curiosity than for any other reason, they had attended Mass, looking in their rich clothes curiously out of place among the peasants and their children.

They drove now to the Padre's house, and when they arrived at the door were told by the servant that he was in the church.

Leaving the car, Fiona and Andrew walked across in the sunshine. After the glare, as they entered the thick oak door, the cool darkness inside was like walking into another world.

There was no one there, save a figure kneeling before the altar.

"It's the Padre," Fiona whispered. "We'll wait for him here."

At last the priest rose from his knees, and turning, saw them waiting for him at the end of the chapel. He walked quickly down to greet them.

He spoke very broken English, but it was enough for them to understand his greeting.

Shyly Fiona explained that she had brought a gift for the church, for him to spend as he would, but at the same time she would like some of it spent on decoration.

"I quite understand," he said.

But when she took out the notes and pressed them into his hand, he stared, amazed at the number.

"How much are you giving me?" he faltered at last,

When Fiona told him the sum he stared at her in amazement.

"It is an answer from God," he said. "There are families around here who will be very hungry this winter. The crops are not good this year. I was praying that they might be helped—and lo! you bring the answer!"

His face, lit up by faith, was a very beautiful thing, and it was almost silently that Fiona and Andrew drove back to Monte Carlo. They felt as though they had been near to something very holy.

Back at the hotel, Andrew sat at his writing-desk and began to write. When Fiona asked him what he was doing, he replied:

"I am making my will, dear. We must go into the town to-morrow and have it properly signed and sealed."

Presently he blotted what he had written and laid it in the blotter.

"I won't read it to you now," he said, "it will be a surprise to-morrow. But Fiona, my dearest, I have made you independent of worry for the rest of your life."

Fiona kissed him gratefully. How wonderful, she thought—no more work, no more anxiety as to where her next meal would come from.

"And now let us go out to-night to celebrate it," he said.

They went to the Casino, and Fiona had a flutter at roulette.

After an hour's hard play, she found herself within a hundred francs of where she started, and laughing she rose from the table.

"I have obviously not gambler's luck, nor ill-luck either," she said. "Let us go and have a drink, and then home. You must be tired, Andrew."

"I am a little to-night," he confessed, "I don't know why; but I am very happy, my darling."

In her sitting-room Fiona raised her face to be kissed.

"Good night," she said, "and I'm terribly happy we gave that money away to-day."

"So am I," Andrew answered. "Good night, my sweet, and God bless you."

He disappeared into his room. Fiona went to hers, but she did not feel really tired. She stood for a while on her balcony.

It was a very hot night, with practically no breeze at all from the sea. Suddenly she felt that she would like to go downstairs and walk by the beach.

She took a dark coat from the wardrobe and put it over her evening dress. She would walk along, she thought, by the beach, safe from any loiterers in the lights of the hotel and those of the Casino, and yet alone, so that she could think.

She felt restless to-night. Some nights the memory of Jim prevented her from sleeping, and this was one of them.

Not only her heart but her body cried out for him and tortured her with memories; the joy in each other, the thrill she had felt in his arms, and the touch of his dear mouth on hers.

She must walk, she must tire herself, before she attempted to sleep, for she knew that she could not rest for some hours.

She rang for the lift, but it was a long time coming, and, eager to be on her way, she did not wait, but ran down the broad staircase which led to the big entrance hall.

As she descended, she saw several people enter, and a porter carrying a suitcase walked across the hall.

"New arrivals," she thought, and hesitated a moment at the bend of the stairs—she did not want to walk straight into them in the doorway.

And then, as she hesitated, her heart gave a great leap. Walking across the hall, accompanied by a woman, was Jim.

For a moment all the blood seemed to drain away from her heart, leaving her faint and shaking, and then, pulling herself together and turning swiftly before anyone saw her, Fiona ran upstairs again.

In her own room, she shut the door, and realised that she was shaking from head to foot. Her hands were damp, and for a moment she felt almost sick with the shock.

She sat down on the bed, and put her face between her hands. What was she to do?

Jim . . . and his wife! Jim and Ann together, somewhere in this hotel, at this moment.

Divided from her by only a few bricks and mortar was Jim . . . the man she loved! She could not meet him . . . could not bear to see him again, and, what was more, she could not let him see her.

Swiftly came the thought.

"What would he think of me and Andrew?"

Would he believe that their association was entirely innocent? Would he believe that the rich clothes and jewels she wore were the gift of a love which gave all and took nothing for itself? Or would he, like the rest of the world around them, believe that she was Andrew's mistress?

Fiona was not so obtuse that she had missed the glances from other women, the underlying insolence of

123

the servants, and the knowing gaze she intercepted from men.

She was quite content to ignore them, thankful that Andrew did not seem to notice them as she did. But with Jim it was different. She could imagine that his wife would not believe her—what other woman would?

Unless she could see Jim alone, how could she explain? And even if she did explain, she could not bear the doubt, or even the jealousy, he might feel.

Somehow Fiona could never for a moment believe that Jim had ceased to love her. She knew that his love was too strong, too true a thing for it to die easily.

She believed implicitly that he loved her still, as she knew she loved him. What was she to do?

She had not told Andrew fully of the depth of her love for Jim. She had told him a little, but perhaps he guessed more than she imagined.

At the same time, it was never easy to tell one man, who loved you, of your affection for another. Fiona could not disguise her true feeling for Jim. Perhaps Andrew guessed a little, perhaps he did not.

Anyway, since she had at first told him a little of her life, Fiona seldom, if ever, referred to Jim in her conversation.

What could she do now, she thought. What could she possibly do? She waited a long while, crept downstairs again. She felt she must clear her brain, she must walk, she must think. The hall was empty and deserted.

She walked steadily along the beach, and finally sat down on a rock, finding the soft lapping of the sea and the solitude around her soothing to her troubled nerves.

She sat there for a long time. After a while she was not consciously thinking at all, she was just letting the waves lap her story to her—the story of herself and Jim.

As he had walked across the hall she knew that her love for him was terrifyingly strong; it was stronger than herself, she could hardly control it.

She knew now she must on no account see him. She must go away.

Dawn was breaking when she went back to the hotel;

the early Mediterranean dawn, rather grey, was creeping up the sky. She went to her room, took off her evening dress and put on a dressing-gown. Then she started to pack.

She packed her things with methodical care. Slowly the pale morning sunshine crept in at the window, then burst over the sea in a blaze of glory. The hotel was already awake and stirring.

Fiona looked in the glass at the deep lines of sleeplessness under her eyes. She walked across the shuttered sitting-room, and paused for a moment outside Andrew's door.

She must awaken him—they must be off before Jim was astir.

Hesitating a moment, then plucking up courage, she knocked tentatively on his door. There was no answer. She knocked again, then turned the handle and walked in.

The room was shuttered to dimness. Fiona pulled back the curtains and opened the shutters. She turned to the bed where Andrew lay. He was very still.

She looked at him again—and then realised that he was dead.

CHAPTER SIX

The doctor, the proprietor—furious that anyone should die in his hotel—curious *femmes de chambre,* valets eager to see if there were any pickings to be sent to relations—

Fiona could never remember afterwards whom she had seen and whom she hadn't, what she had done and what she had not done.

All she could understand was that Andrew, her dear Andrew who loved her, was dead; dead in a strange hotel, where only she knew him well.

He had died with a smile on his lips, and Fiona was glad that their last night together had been such a happy one.

"The last month of his life was one of happiness," she told herself. "I have nothing to regret."

The doctor, who was French, was very kind and understanding. It was he who took most of the arrangements out of her hands.

"We must find out if his family wish him to be sent home," he said. "Do not worry, dear *Madame,* I will arrange everything for you."

Finally, Fiona went to her room, at his insistence, and taking the sleeping-draught he gave her, lay down and slept.

She awoke three or four hours later, and it was afternoon. There was a tap at the door, and a boy brought her a message from the doctor, to say that he had received a telegram from Mrs. Uckfield that she was starting at once for Monte Carlo.

Fiona rose from her bed, her head still a little stupid from the effect of the sleeping-draught, and finding her bag, opened it for a franc to give the boy.

It was only as she did so that a sudden thought made her stand so still that the boy, thinking she had forgotten him, coughed sharply.

Hastily she pushed two francs into his hand, and with a swift *"Merci, Madame,"* he went from the room, slamming the door behind him.

Alone, Fiona stared at her bag again, and slowly took out the notes it contained. Five hundred francs and some loose change—that was all she possessed in cash in the world.

She went to the blotter in the sitting-room and, opening it, found the will Andrew had made the night before.

When she read it, she felt a warm glow of gratitude towards him for all that he had meant to do for her.

He had left her eight hundred pounds a year for life, the money to be held in trust for her, so that the capital should not be dissipated.

"Dear Andrew!" she thought.

At the same time came the sickening certainty that she would never get the money now.

Fiona was not a fool. She knew she might expect no kindness at the hands of Mrs. Uckfield. Andrew had never found fault with or abused his wife in any way, but Fiona knew all too well the type of woman she was.

No woman could have lived for thirty-five years with Andrew Uckfield and not found out the charm and kindliness of his character, unless she were an extraordinarily hard person.

Fiona had a very good notion of Mrs. Uckfield's idea of the type of girl who would live with her husband in the South of France.

Lancashire born and bred, she would have the narrow, rigid conventions of the North Country.

Fiona knew that no explanation could possible convince her that a girl who allowed Andrew Uckfield to support her was anything less than a harlot.

The proprietor had not been too pleasant in his observations to Fiona.

He also had his theories as to women who lived on the bounty of rich men—not that they did not have their uses. He was delighted so long as they brought business to his hotel, but in the capacity of a scandal, they were not only useless but a danger to him.

He had hinted to Fiona that it would be better if her room was vacated before Mrs. Uckfield arrived, and the doctor had put it even more plainly to her.

He had asked Fiona outright if the dead man's wife had known of her presence, and when she shook her head, he said:

"*Ma chère, Madame,* if you take my advice, she will never know."

Fiona, in spite of her misery, could not help smiling at the graceful way the French arranged these things. But she felt certain they were right. There was no point in making Mrs. Uckfield unhappy now.

The trouble was, how was she to find money to live?

She had no idea, and then she remembered the diamond bracelet and the brooch which Andrew had given her.

She decided finally to go back to England;—Jim was here, with his wife—there, would be no chance of running into them.

Anyway, now he was married, her original idea of leaving him had borne the fruit, bitter though it was, that she had intended.

He had not sought her out—he had married Ann, and she was an episode in his life which had only to be forgotten.

Late that afternoon Fiona left the hotel. Before she left, she tore up the will which Andrew had made, and which without his signature was utterly valueless.

She looked round to see that every trace of herself had vanished, even taking the women's papers from the sitting-room.

She deposited her luggage at the station, and then walked into the town.

Dusk was falling, and already the little lights in the brightly flowered gardens which climb the hill opposite the Winter Casino, were shining, looking like tiny fairy globes among the brilliant blossoms around them.

Slowly Fiona walked up to where the brightly lit jewellery shops advertised their wares by flaring white arc lamps, which made the stones glitter and shimmer as though they were alive.

Somewhat nervously, she entered a shop near the Casino, and offered the man behind the counter her brooch.

Only two weeks previously, Andrew had paid ten thousand francs for it, but now she was offered two thousand five hundred.

When Fiona expostulated, the man laughed, and said he must make a profit some way or another, and that the season was short.

Too sick at heart to argue, and hating the whole transaction, Fiona agreed, and he handed her the notes across the counter.

She still had the bracelet left, she thought, and she could dispose of that when she got to London, where the jewellers were fairer and she was likely to get a better price.

However, she was economical on her journey, travelling second-class, sitting upright in the train as it wound its way round the Corniche road till it finally swept away from the sea and she knew that her holiday on the Riviera was over.

She had a bad crossing of the Channel, and arrived at Dover feeling sick and dishevelled. It was raining when she arrived, yet somehow that fact was comforting.

She was home again, home in England with its bad weather and very likely its bad times for her.

In a third-class carriage, packed with people, smoking, hot, it was difficult to believe that but a few days ago she was sitting in a Hispano-Suiza, with money being showered on her by someone who loved her.

She closed her eyes and tried to imagine it.

The only thing she could see vividly was Andrew, lying still and stiff in his bed when she had gone to his room that morning.

The arrival at Victoria was indeed a homecoming. The noise, the shouting of paper-boys, the gloom and the dirty pavements outside—she was home.

She wondered where she was to stay that night. Her flat was given up, and she had no friends to whom to turn.

Finally she drove to a tiny hotel that she knew near Victoria, small, very noisy, and not very clean, but at least she knew where she was.

There were no unknown dangers, it was just England and all that England stood for to her, hard work and the never-ceasing necessity of finding food.

She managed to get a little supper from her landlady, but it was not very appetising, and she left most of it untouched.

She felt utterly lonely, and wondered to whom she could speak. Anyone, she thought, would be better than no one—even someone she disliked.

Then she laughed aloud at the mere idea.

Suddenly she thought of Donald. She would ring him up.

The telephone was of the antiquated kind, set on the wall in the narrow hall which gave access to the bar, and the noise of the customers completely prevented the person speaking from hearing anything else.

However, nothing daunted, she rang up Donald's newspaper office, and asked to speak to him.

After a long, long wait, a voice asked if it was a personal call or if she had news.

Fiona knew this trick of old, and firmly she said she had news, but could give it to no one else. After another long wait, she heard Donald's voice at the end of the line.

"Donald," she said, "it's Fiona."

"Fiona!" She heard his note of excitement. "Fiona, is it really you? What has happened to you? Where have you been?"

"Oh, Donald," she said, "I've had so many adventures! I do so want to see you."

"I must see you to-morrow," he said. "Where can I meet you?"

She gave him the address of her hotel, and he promised to come and see her about one o'clock the following day.

"I can't talk now," he added, "I'm on a job, and I must go off."

"All right," Fiona said, "I quite understand. Good night, Donald, dear. I've lots to tell you."

'At least I have one friend,' she thought.

Feeling happier, she went up to her small bedroom and, in spite of the hardness of the bed, fell into a peaceful slumber.

Next morning she was ready and waiting for Donald a good half-hour before he appeared. There was something very thrilling about seeing him again.

When she saw him coming towards her, her first impression was one of surprise. She had forgotten how terribly shabby and down-at-heel Donald looked.

Her eyes had become accustomed to rich men and rich men's clothing. She had often thought of Donald, and yet when he came towards her she found that she had forgotten so much about him.

It was with gladness in her voice that she spoke his name and held out her hand, and felt it clutched in both of his, held on to as though he would never let her go again.

After many greetings and explanations, they finally went out to find a quiet place to lunch.

It was then, over luncheon, that Fiona tried to tell Donald a little of what she had been through, yet the words stuck in her throat.

She could not speak to Donald of Jim, and somehow she felt she could not tell him the true story of Andrew.

131

Hurriedly she skirted her tale, telling him this and that, and somehow avoiding the main issues.

"How smart you look, Fiona," Donald said.

Fiona, glancing at the looking-glass opposite, realised that indeed she was a different person from the girl he last saw.

Her little hat, pulled over one eye, was the very last word in French millinery, her dress, so simple to the inexperienced eye, was a triumph of Chanel's art, and cost more than Donald would earn in three months.

"Don't talk about me," said Fiona, feeling a little self-conscious and ashamed of the extravagance of her garments. "Tell me about yourself. What have you done, Donald?"

It was then Donald blushed crimson, and averted his eyes from hers.

"Fiona, I've lost your money!" he stammered.

For a moment Fiona was silent.

She had always thought that sooner or later Donald would repay that money, and it would be a nest-egg, as she had originally intended it to be, against really abject penury.

"It doesn't matter, Donald," she said quickly. "I've got lots of money. I was going to make you a present of it, anyway."

"Were you really, Fiona?" Donald's face lit up again. "But is that honestly true? Have you got lots of money?"

"Lots," Fiona lied. "Don't you think I'm looking rich?"

"But—" Donald hesitated, and she knew he was thinking of her hotel.

"I was so tired last night," Fiona said before he could speak, "that I went to the first hotel the taximan took me to."

It was a feeble lie, but it sufficed.

"Oh, Fiona, I'm so relieved!" Donald said. "I've been through hell, wondering what to do about that money."

"Tell me about it," Fiona said gently.

"My brother lost in the end," Donald said. "It was

all much worse than I knew—I can't tell you about it, Fiona. He got four years' imprisonment. It very nearly killed my mother."

"Poor Donald!" Fiona said, putting out a hand and touching his arm. "I am so sorry. But please, don't worry about my money."

"Fiona—" Donald said.

"You're not to think about it again," Fiona went on.

"You're an angel," Donald answered, squeezing her hand. "Things are so difficult at the moment. I didn't sleep a wink last night, wondering how I was going to tell you, and trying to think how I could possibly repay you, if you had rung me up to ask me for the money."

"How silly you are!" Fiona laughed. "As though you couldn't tell me anything. But why are things difficult apart from that?"

"Well, my mother's been ill," he said, "and I've had to move her into London. She's living with me now, so that she can have the treatment the doctor insists on. My wages don't go very far."

He smiled.

"That's always the way, isn't it?" Fiona laughed back. "I remember, in the old days!"

Still playing the lady bountiful, she insisted on paying for luncheon. She had changed her remaining francs into pounds earlier that morning, and she watched one of her notes go now with a little apprehensive quiver.

"Oh, dear!" she thought. "My life seems to be perpetually being absolutely penniless or living in the lap of luxury! If only it could be half-way between the two, for a change!"

Then she reproved herself for complaining.

"Mediocrity is always dull—at least my life isn't boring, whatever else it is!"

On an impulse, she took a pound note from her bag, and when Donald left her insisted on giving it to him.

"It's for your mother," she said; "you can't refuse a present for your mother. You must get her something that she really wants, some luxury that she wouldn't have otherwise."

While he stammered his thanks, she waved her hand to him and walked away.

'I've enjoyed so much luxury,' she thought to herself. 'I'm not certain that the extravagant things of this life aren't more of a tonic to people that haven't got them, than all the doctors' medicine in the world.'

And so philosophising, she entered a large pawnbroker's, slipping as she did so her diamond bracelet from her arm.

At the pawnbroker's she had a disappointment.

She had hoped to get a good deal on her diamond bracelet, for the jeweler in Monte Carlo had charged Andrew an exorbitantly high price for its flashing beauty.

Eighty-five pounds was what the pawnbroker offered her if she wished him to purchase it outright, and forty-five if she desired only to pawn it.

When she argued, he pointed out that the stones were small and of not the best quality, that there was very little genuine platinum used in the setting, and that as a "break-up" piece it was worth considerably less than he was offering her.

In fact, after twenty minutes' conversation, Fiona almost believed that the gentleman in possession was doing her a magnificent service in condescending to purchase her jewellery at all.

Finally she was obliged to accept the eighty-five pounds he offered her.

She did not go back to Chelsea and ask if her old flat was still free.

She decided that for the present it would be wiser to take a bedroom nearer the part of London where she intended to hunt for a job.

Accordingly, she moved her luggage and herself to a small quiet hotel off Oxford Street. It was uninviting, being used almost exclusively by commercials, but it was respectable and central.

Fiona went first to the school of dancing where she

had worked in the summer months, but her abrupt departure without notice ensured her a very poor welcome.

There was no vacancy, she was told, and received the impression that even had there been one, she would not have been given the chance of obtaining it.

She visited several establishments which catered for afternoon or evening classes, but the busy season had not yet begun, and anyway they did not seem over-enthusiastic about engaging a girl, however good-looking, with no particular references, and whose chief ability seemed to be a strong desire for immediate work.

Fiona spent two days wandering from place to place, following up even the vaguest suggestions, culled from anyone, as to where there might be an opportunity.

She asked everyone she met if they had heard of anything—commissionaires, proprietors, girls already working, those who like herself were on the lookout.

She began to see that her task was not going to be as easy as she had hoped, and rigidly she began to curtail her daily expenditure, cutting down her meals to a minimum, spending as little on fares as she could.

She was just beginning to get slightly disheartened on the third day of her quest, when walking down Oxford Street she saw a familiar figure advancing towards her.

Slightly overdressed, with a bowler hat tilted at a provocative angle on his black hair, she recognised the jaunty carriage and sulky good looks of Paul.

"Fiona!" he exclaimed, as they advanced towards each other, "by all that's wonderful! What are you doing here?"

His quick glance took in every detail of her smart black dress, expensive fur and chic hat. It did not miss her 100-guage stockings, well-cut shoes and unworn gloves.

His hand-clasp became warmer, his smile more gracious, and he pressed her to come and have some luncheon with him and tell her news.

Nothing loath, but wise enough to be slightly evasive

in her preliminary answers, Fiona allowed herself to be taken to a small quiet lunch place near by.

Here, seated at a table, choosing with care from the tempting menu, she could not help smiling a little to herself at the attention Paul was giving her because of her good clothes.

She liked Paul, but had no illusions as to the complete selfishness of his outlook on life. He valued everyone from the point of view as to whether they would be useful to him.

He was inordinately curious, and he could hardly wait now in his eagerness to question Fiona as to what she had been doing.

He was unaffectedly glad at her success, which was one of the things which made him likeable, even weighed singly against all his other faults.

"Tell me everything," he kept saying, "how smart you are—where have you come from? Tell me more. What have you done all the summer? What are you going to do now?"

Fiona told him a reasonable and concise story. She omitted Jim altogether, but mentioned Andrew as having given her a very lovely time and as having meant a great deal in her life.

She also mentioned that he was dead, and Paul was immediately very sympathetic.

"And now—what do you intend to do now?" Paul asked, and then Fiona, as she sipped her coffee, decided to tell him the truth.

"I have got to find a job, you see, Paul. I have come back to London with very little money. "I've got a few pounds to keep me until I can find a job, but I've got to work, and the sooner I find it the better.

"Can you help me, Paul? What are you doing yourself? Are you still at Paglioni's?"

"But it's too fortunate!" Paul said eagerly, bending forward in his excitement until his handsome face was within a few inches of Fiona's. "It's a chance—no, absolute fate!—that made me walk down Oxford Street this morning.

"Listen, Fiona. I have just agreed to take up the position of dance instructor at a new and very smart club which is opening near here. It's to be *the* Mayfair night club. All smart Society will go there.

"Of course, it is not a restaurant. There's no dinner—only supper, and the place won't start until after eleven o'clock. In fact, it will not really get going until one or two in the morning.

"Rather late hours, perhaps, but at the same time immensely lucrative, for one will meet the smartest and richest people there.

"Americans, tourists, and people of that sort will go there, besides the people you and I are so used to seeing—the smart crowd. Tips will not only be allowed, but will be essential.

"You ought to clear ten pounds a week easily if you try, and there will also be a percentage on the drinks which you sell personally.

"Dancing lessons can be given in the daytime, and I personally expect to do very well out of them."

Paul gave a little smirk, and Fiona wondered how often his lessons were genuine, or merely an excuse.

However, she was very excited at his news, and very grateful to him when he promised that not only should she be dance-hostess at the place he mentioned, but that she should also be more or less his permanent partner.

They would start the evening and, it might be, giving an occasional exhibition dance if it were required of them, and no other cabaret turns were forthcoming.

"It's quite easy," he assured her. "We can easily work up a tango together, and an exhibition valse. At that time of the night people are not particular, and it pleases the management to think they are getting a cabaret free occasionally."

Fiona agreed, and they pledged her acceptance of his offer in a glass of port.

She spent the next three or four days before the club opened in finding herself a small room as near as possible.

If she were unable to leave until three or four in the morning there would be no chance of her returning home by any other means of transport than a taxi.

If she could be within walking distance, or at any rate a very small fare, it was going to be both convenient and economical.

After trying several places for a room, she finally went to a block of flatlets to which Paul recommended her.

"They are not over-respectable," he said, "but what does it matter? Why should that affect you? They are comfortable and well run and not in a noisy neighbourhood. That is important if you have to sleep a good part of the day."

Fiona agreed, and when she saw the flatlet—which was very aptly described, for it was quite the smallest place imaginable—she decided that it would suit her needs admirably.

The small room was divided into a bed-sitting room at one end, and at the other, partitioned off, was a tiny kitchenette.

There was running water, an electric fire and a telephone, and the bathroom was only a floor below.

She was high up, and the windows looked out on to a dusty, dingly but deserted square. There was a self-working lift, and the landlord promised that the water was constantly hot.

The whole thing cost twenty-five shillings a week, but in such a neighbourhood Fiona decided that this was cheap, and she felt she could leave it at any time should she have less or more money to spend.

The New Broadway Club opened with a tremendous flourish on a Wednesday night.

Very little had been spent on the decoration of an underground room, containing neither windows, nor, as far as Fiona could ascertain, any ventilation.

The walls were painted a bright green, and a few mirrors broke the similarity of their surface.

Fiona first went there in the afternoon, when the

lights were unshaded and some semblance of daylight filtered in through a skylight in one corner of the room.

She was horrified at what she saw: the chairs piled one on each other gave a desolate, mournful look; the bare tables without their cloths and with wine-stains on their tops, and with chipped legs, were only more pathetic to see than the almost threadbare carpet which surrounded the dance floor.

The patches of damp which stained the ceiling were matched by the dust and refuse which, in the strong light, were painfully apparent in the corners of the room.

"Surely this isn't likely to be a place for really smart people?" she asked Paul, but he laughed.

"You bet your life!" he said. "It looks pretty lousy now, but wait till it's got all its war paint on!"

The manager liked Fiona, her looks and manner, and told Paul so on his first introduction. After a quick appraising look, he held out his hand.

"Okay! She'll do us fine—just what we wanted, eh, Paul?"

And there passed between them a quick look of understanding.

Fiona's first bad impression of the club was quickly swept away when she entered it on its opening night.

She was of course early, a little excited and flurried as to whether the whole thing would be the success which Paul and its manager anticipated.

When she arrived there was no one there. She had entered by the customers' entrance, a door guarded by a huge commissionaire and a small man at a desk, with a list of members before him.

Fiona ran downstairs, and then, as she entered the dance room, she looked round and realised that Paul had been quite right.

The lights were cunningingly lowered, until the whole place seemed like a cave, dark, cool and suggestive. Little orange lights flickered enticingly on every table.

The dance floor was of glass and lit from beneath

with deep coloured lights, which could alter and change as the tunes varied.

In this atmosphere it was quite impossible to see either the dirt or dinginess of the carpet and sofas.

The tables were all concealed by bright orange cloths and were gay with highly polished glass and bright green napkins.

The manager was moving swiftly here and there, giving final instructions to a large number of waiters as they passed to and from the serving room.

Fiona saw that rows and rows of bottles had already been taken from the cellars below, and were stacked just inside the service door, ready for the customers' demands.

She had asked Paul about extensions, and he had replied that by law they were only allowed one extension a week, but that he hoped drinking would be extended more often than that, or else their percentage would not be a large item.

"As long as we don't go to prison, I don't mind," Fiona had answered.

She knew that places of this kind were in continual warfare with the police in their efforts to continue selling alcohol long after hours.

"That's all right for you, Fiona," Paul had assured her. "You stick to your dancing, and no one can say a word."

By twelve o'clock the place was full, and yet people continued to arrive until after three o'clock. At four in the morning it was still comparatively crowded.

The members of the band smiled continually and their crooning voices never stopped, inciting the well-dressed crowd to revolve ceaselessly on the coloured glass floor.

Fiona had never seen so much liquor consumed before. The manager was continuously going down to the cellars to superintend another lot of bottles being brought upstairs.

After three o'clock the champagne was emptied into jugs and brought to the tables disguised, as it were, in cups.

Fiona had a feeling that this was not so much to deceive the police—which, had they raided the club, it would never have done—but rather to disguise from the customers that while they were paying a vintage price they were receiving the very cheapest form of champagne procurable.

Most of the customers, however, by this time were not in a state to recognise one brand from another. With flushed faces they sat amourously affectionate, or swayed in locked embrace on the closely packed floor.

It was a very tired girl who finally reached her tiny flatlet room at a quarter past five. Already the milkman and the dustman were starting on their rounds.

Fiona's feet ached, and her eyes were dropping with sleep as she reached home, and even yet the club had not actually closed.

The manager, Paul and the waiters were concerned with locking it up, and seeing the band and the kitchen staff off the premises.

"What a night!" Fiona said to herself. "I suppose I shall get used to these late hours."

She was so tired when she got into bed that she could not sleep for a little while. In her head echoed continuously the tunes to which she had been listening for the last six hours.

"What a way to live!" she thought again.

Then gradually the peace of her room and the softness of her bed lulled her to sleep.

She dreamt of Jim.

*　　*　　*

Fiona continued for the next two months as dance hostess of the New Broadway Club.

To begin with, the club had a meteoric success. It got a good deal of "gossip" press, for according to them —"Mayfair's brightest and smartest set" were there night after night.

It was towards Christmas-time that a change seemed to come over the place.

Up to that time it had been very smart, fashionable, and at times rather noisily drunken. Fiona had found that Paul had not exaggerated when he told her she might make ten pounds a week.

Her tips very often exceeded this, and to her joy she had very little trouble with men running after her.

She became quite friendly with some of them, and used to accept invitations to luncheon, although taking good care that such invitations she accepted were written legibly in their engagement books.

This was after two or three times of finding herself stranded at a fashionable restaurant on the day following the invitation.

However, Fiona discovered that although her wages reached such unprecedented heights, her expenses, as she had anticipated, were also very heavy.

Her dress bill was enormous. Dresses could not last for long the congestion on the dance floor, and the clumsy handling they too often received from over-elated partners.

The rule of the club was gaiety, and nearly every night the band spurred its patrons to wilder and wilder dancing, to the tunes of older days.

It was all very harmless, and quite amusing at the time, but it had a devastating effect upon fragile evening frocks.

Fiona found that while her dress bill was big her cleaning bill was even bigger, and though she obtained theatrical rates, the sum that she paid weekly was quite considerable.

She had been asked particularly by the management not to wear black dresses more often than she could help.

Black was considered depressing, and the manager's taste ran to white or bright colours, which showed up well in the room and which drew attention to Fiona herself.

About Christmas-time she noticed that several new members were becoming habitués of the club, and these seemed rather a different type from any of the previous ones.

There was a dark man, always beautifully dressed, but with something unusual and unpleasant about him, which could not entirely be accounted for by the fact that he had a slight squint.

He was always with other men, and never seemed to have any use for or take any interest in the women.

He drank sparingly, in fact some nights he would have nothing but a bottle of mineral water, and yet, to Fiona's surprise, both the manager and Paul treated him with great deference.

He seemed particularly interested in Paul, and they would often have long talks together, though the subject of their conversation was a continual mystery.

Paul even deserted some of his own clients to talk to this man, whose name, Fiona afterwards heard was Heimer—Dr. Heimer, though what he was a doctor of was again wrapped in mystery.

Every night he would come to the club about eleven-thirty and stay until nearly three. He would watch the people dancing, watch those sitting at the tables, in a quiet analytical fashion.

When the New Broadway Club had started it was considered imperative that evening dress should be essential, but now two or three people began to be allowed in in ordinary clothes, and, so slowly as to be at first imperceptible, the *chic* atmosphere began to alter.

It was just as gay, just as crowded, but the people were less the Smart Set, though they seemed to have an equal amount of high spirits and apparently just as much money to spend.

The change happened so slowly that at first Fiona hardly noticed it, and then suddenly one night she looked around at Dr. Heimer in the corner, at the two strange women in their usual seat, and she noted the difference.

There was a lack of smart people, many were not in evening dress, and the large number one could imagine nowhere else except in a low-lighted, under-ventilated night club.

'I wonder why,' she thought, and made up her mind to ask Paul.

She saw so little of Paul these days. He seemed to her to have got thinner, but at the same time to be more vivacious and better dressed than ever. There was no doubt of his attraction for women of every age.

To-night Fiona sat at her table hoping that Paul would return for a few moments, so that she could speak to him.

She noticed that he was dancing with a large, fat woman with whom he seemed rather bored, and she hoped that he might seize an opportunity to escape if she were sitting alone.

Sure enough, her anticipation was right, and in a few moments Paul came across to her and sat down, wiping his forehead with a handkerchief.

"Phew!" he said, "it's hot, and that awful old tank I had to dance with was like a sack of coals. Such woman ought not to be allowed to exist."

Fiona laughed.

"You didn't look as though you were enjoying it."

"Didn't I?" he exclaimed, looking for a moment genuinely concerned. "I must be more careful. It's the greatest mistake ever to look bored. It puts other people off."

Fiona smiled at his serious vanity.

"Never mind," she said, "there doesn't seem any slackening in your numbers."

"Did I really look bored?" he said to her again, and then he rose to his feet.

"Don't go," Fiona said quickly, "I want to talk to you."

"Wait a moment," he replied, "I'll be back in a second. Will you order me a brandy and soda?"

Fiona nodded, and called a waiter; Paul had disappeared down the passage towards the gentlemen's cloakroom.

He was away about five minutes, and when he returned he was in much better spirits.

"He really is extraordinarily handsome," she told herself, "with those dark, flashing eyes and rather clearly cut features, combined with his breadth and height and graceful carriage."

Paul suddenly seemed in tremendously good spirits thereafter, and talked and enjoyed his drink, and finally, in spite of her remonstrances, insisted on dancing with Fiona.

They passed Dr. Heimer as they danced, and Paul waved him a greeting.

With the minimum of expression, Dr. Heimer conveyed to Paul that he wished to speak to him, and Paul nodded in assent, and danced Fiona back towards their table.

"I hate that man," Fiona said, as they stopped dancing. "Why are you such friends with him, Paul?"

But Paul did not answer. He gave her a strange look, shrugged his shoulders, and picked his way through the crowd back to Dr. Heimer's table.

The club had been going nearly four months, and the manager—Fiona surmised—could not help but be surprised that up to now, in spite of the lax observance of the drinking regulations, they had not been raided.

Whether it was bribery or just luck Fiona was not in a position to judge, although she had her suspicions as to what method was adopted to keep Society's playground intact.

Just lately a new lavatory attendant had been engaged, and Fiona had taken a most unreasonable dislike to him.

Of course she did not see much of him, but he had a habit of standing at the door which led into the gentlemen's cloakroom, and leering out at the people passing up and down the stairs.

"I can't bear that new man," she told Paul casually, after striving to conceal her dislike for nearly a week.

"He's quite all right," Paul said in an almost hostile manner.

145

"Oh, I'm sure he is," Fiona answered; "it's just that I'm fanciful about it. At the same time, I can't help it—I have an overwhelming abhorrence of him."

"Well, I think that's extremely silly," Paul said tersely.

Rising to his feet he left her sitting at the table, surprised at his abrupt manner.

"Why should he mind my disliking one of the club servants?" Fiona asked herself.

Then, as there was no one to answer it, she left the questions unsolved, and rose to dance with an old man who should have been in bed hours ago.

About three evenings later, Fiona came to the club feeling curiously tired and dispirited.

She did not know why, but lately she had found it more and more difficult to work herself up to the gaiety and infectious merriment which she knew was required of her as a stimulus to the guests.

To-night she had a headache, and she walked wearily from her room to the club.

Downstairs everything was as usual. The waiters were setting the tables, and the band had just arrived and were tuning up with the usual maddening repetitive note which is synonymous with such action.

Fiona was early, and she wondered if Paul had yet arrived.

She asked one of the waiters, who said he thought he had seen him a few minutes ago going into the manager's office, and Fiona decided she would go there to see.

She went through the service door, turning to the left down a short, dark passage, and walked towards the small cubbyhole which was used as the manager's office and where also the safe was kept.

As she neared the door, she heard voices, and one sentence came suddenly to her ears:

"You must be careful, I tell you," she heard the manager say. "You are taking unnecessary risks, Paul, and you will land us all in prison."

"But I've got to have it, I tell you!" Fiona heard Paul reply. "I've got to—and the other poor devils are more desperate than I am."

Realising she was eavesdropping, Fiona instinctively stepped backwards, hesitated a moment, and then retraced her steps to the dance room.

Somehow she didn't want either Paul or the manager to know that she had heard what they said. At the same time, her brain was busy with what she had heard.

What risks was Paul taking, and why would they land him in prison? She supposed it was the drink, and yet there had been a strange ring in Paul's voice when he had said, "I tell you I've got to have it."

Got to have what? Surely there was no difficulty for him in having any drink he wanted.

He at any rate ran no risk, because he could always go to the manager's office and drink there without paying and without therefore running any legal risk.

Fiona was still worried over what she had heard, and Paul and the manager had not appeared when singly and in couples the patrons began to come in. There was a gloomy atmosphere about them to-night.

Some days it was like that, sometimes the place seemed a riot of youth and gaiety, at other times there was a heavy intangible depression hanging over the whole place which all the efforts of the band and endless bottles of champagne could not lift.

To-night must be one of what Fiona termed to herself the "bad nights."

However, by twelve o'clock things had improved a little.

Just before midnight Dr. Heimer arrived, walking slowly and with dignity, as usual accompanied by another man as reserved as himself, and of unnoticeable appearance.

No sooner was he seated in his usual place than Paul hurried across to him, and Fiona could see they were having a long animated conversation—a conversation

147

in which Paul seemed to do most of the talking, while Dr. Heimer sat immobile staring straight before him.

Fiona was dancing busily for the next hour or so. When she had finally returned to her table it was to find Paul in high good spirits.

She was going to say something about the gloominess of the evening, but when she saw him so happy she thought it better to remain silent.

She was just going to speak when a strange woman came up to the table. She bent over and whispered in his ear, but the band was at that moment playing very softly, and Fiona was able to catch the words.

"Any hope?" she asked.

"As usual," Paul answered.

With a swift smile, which seemed eager and grateful, the woman turned and walked quickly from the room.

Fiona was just going to ask what she had meant, when something in Paul's face stopped her. After all, it was no business of hers.

"Come and dance," Paul said.

In a moment they were swinging together rhythmically over the floor. Fiona always enjoyed dancing with Paul.

He was a perfect dancer, and as they moved together she half shut her eyes, enjoying the unrestricted movement and the pleasure it gave her to be dancing with someone who was a professional.

Then, one moment she was dancing and the next moment standing alone bewildered, even shaken—what had happened?

As she wondered, the band stopped playing with a sudden crash, and she looked up to see a large number of policemen, some in plain clothes and some in uniform, entering the room.

Paul had disappeared. A woman screamed near her, and a man next to her said,

"Of all the damnable luck—a raid! The only night I've been here for months!"

148

To Fiona's surprise, however, the police seemed to take no notice of the drink lying on the tables.

They looked quickly round the room, and then two of them advanced to Dr. Heimer, who had risen in his seat, and, after a quiet word with him, he walked down the room between them.

Fiona watched with surprise, and then suddenly came a voice in her ear.

"We want a few words with you, please, Miss," and she found a constable beside her.

"With me?" she said in surprise, but she followed him outside into the vestibule.

Names and addresses of all the people present were being taken, and as she passed it seemed to Fiona that they were being taken in a somewhat perfunctory fashion.

She had the idea that it was not drink they were after, but something else, and when she got outside she was not surprised to see that the lavatory attendant for whom she had taken so great a dislike was standing guarded by two policemen.

An inspector was waiting there.

"Where is Paul Rattain?" he asked the policeman who was escorting Fiona.

"He's not inside," was the answer, and the inspector turned to her.

"Do you know where he is?"

"No," replied Fiona.

"Has he been here this evening?"

"Yes," she answered.

She was just going to add that he was actually dancing with her when the police entered, but something stopped her.

If Paul was in trouble and had made a get-away, it was not for her to assist the police against him.

The manager and Dr. Heimer were both guarded by policemen.

After a curt word from the inspector they were taken upstairs and out of the building. Fiona was taken by the inspector into a small room which opened out of the vestibule and was used sometimes as an extra store-room.

With him were two other men, obviously detectives.

"What is it? What's happened?" Fiona asked.

"I want you to answer a few questions," the inspector replied, and her answers were recorded in his book.

The police apparently were very anxious to find Paul, but according to them, there was no sign of him in the building, and Fiona wondered how on earth he could have escaped.

They asked Fiona if she knew his address, and she gave it.

She was unable to answer a lot of their questions as to his habits and the people he knew, and finally they questioned her as to her own part in the running of the club.

She told them her hours and arrangements as dance-hostess, and they nodded as though her answers were what they expected.

"She knows nothing," at length one of the detectives said.

"About what?" she asked. "Why do you want Paul, and what is this all about?"

"Did you know," the inspector asked her severely, "that dope trafficking was going on in this club?"

"Dope?" Fiona said in surprise.

Then she understood that her suspicions of the past few weeks had not been without foundation.

So that was what Paul was risking, and that was what she had disliked in Dr. Heimer and the new lavatory attendant!

Her surprise, however, convinced them of what they already knew more or less to be true, and she was told that she could go home.

"You are not to leave London, and you must report at the police station to-morrow morning at ten-thirty," the inspector told her, and she promised to obey.

Fiona hastened home through the empty streets, too

agitated to do anything but get as quickly as she could away from the club.

How had they been so stupid as to get mixed up in this sort of thing, she wondered. No wonder the clientele had changed!

Thank heaven she knew nothing about it, and the police had believed her. And then the sudden thought came to her—surely she was being followed.

She glanced back over her shoulder, and noticed a man a short way behind her. She had an uneasy feeling, a strange conviction that he was not an ordinary foot-passenger.

When she got to the doorway that led to her flat, she waited a little in the shadow—sure enough, he approached quietly, stopped on the other side of the road, and lit a cigarette.

They hadn't been as trusting as she thought, she said to herself uneasily, and then wondered why she should be frightened. After all, she had nothing to fear—she was indeed innocent.

Then the thought struck her—they were after Paul!

She was frightened as she climbed the stairs. Perhaps he would telephone to her—in that she thought she was safe. The house was very quiet and still.

There seemed to be no one moving to-night, and the lights under most of the small flat doors she passed were out.

When she got to her own door, she opened it gently, and then her heart leapt as she saw that the light was on.

She entered, and though the room was empty she had an instinctive impression that someone had been there.

She stood uncertain in the doorway, too frightened to close it.

"Who's here?" she said at last, in a voice just above a whisper.

She came further into the room, but she still had that uneasy feeling that she was not alone.

"Who is here?" she repeated. "I am alone."

The door leading into the partitioned-off kitchen

151

moved slightly, and, as Fiona put her hand against her heart, stifling an inclination to scream, it slowly opened and she saw Paul.

"Paul!" she whispered, and he signalled her to shut the door.

She did so, and pushed the small bolt.

"The police are after you," she said.

"I know that," he said, also in a whisper. "Who have they got?"

He came into the room, as she bent down and turned on the electric fire. She told him whom she had seen them taking away, and then looked up at him.

He was looking dreadfully haggard and quite unlike his usual smart self. His hair was tousled, there was a long scar on his cheek which had bled slightly, and his hands and clothes were dusty and dirty.

"How did you get away?" Fiona asked.

"I got out through the kitchen window," he answered, "and climbed along the waterpipe into the yard of the next building, climbed over the wall and got away. I realised that the police would be watching every other entrance, and waiting for me at home.

"I had to go somewhere, and yours was the nearest place. I'm sorry, Fiona—I didn't want to get you into trouble, but I've got to get away. I must get out of the country. I shall get a long stretch for this otherwise."

"Oh Paul, why did you do it?" Fiona said.

"It was that swine Heimer," he answered. "He started it. He let me taste the damned stuff, and now I can't live without it. Thank God I got some from him to-night, otherwise I should have been more desperate than I am.

"In another week. I should have made enough money to clear out and go abroad for some time. As it is, I've got to go off now without a bean, in fear of my life. How much money have you got?"

Fiona's heart jumped. "I can let you have a little," she said.

"First of all," Paul said, "tell me how I can get out of this place."

152

Fiona thought.

"There's a detective watching the front door," she said.

"I guessed that would happen. Where's the back?"

"It's a front basement," she replied.

"And the fire-escape?"

"That's on the other side of the house—I know, because they showed it me particularly when I came here. You can get on to it from any landing window, but there's a drop of about thirty-feet at the end."

"I can manage that," Paul replied. "What does it drop into."

"I think it drops into the kitchen yard," she replied, "and that leads into a small mews at the back. I should think you could get away from there if they haven't put anyone on to watch."

"I'll have a damn good try," Paul replied; "and what about this money?"

With a sinking heart, Fiona unlocked her trunk and searched for a small jewel box which she kept at the bottom. She wished now that she had put her money away in the bank.

She had over ninety pounds in her box, and though she was quite prepared to give Paul twenty, she wondered how she could distract his attention from the large amount she had with her.

Taking the box on her knees, she sat down facing him, hoping to conceal from him how much it contained.

"How much do you want?" she said.

"How much have you got?" he answered.

"Shall I lend you twenty-five pounds, Paul?" she said gently.

"How much have you got?" he repeated almost roughly, and as she turned the key in the lock and opened the lid of the box, he bent over and put his hand in and took out the packet of notes.

"God, you're a millionairess, girl!" he said swiftly, and licking his finger, began counting the notes, "Ninety-three pounds! Well, that ought to see me on my way."

"But Paul," Fiona cried, "I can't led you all that! That's all I have in the world—and I'm penniless now, too!"

Paul hesitated a moment, then he took a five-pound note and handed it to her.

"Sorry, kid," he said, "but I can't let you have any more. I've got to get out of the country, and God knows when I shall have a chance of making any."

"But Paul—" Fiona expostulated, and then was silent as he looked at her.

"It's no use making a fuss," he said. You know I'm going to have it, and you might just as well take it quietly. One day I may get a chance of repaying you, but it's no use making a scene now—I'm up against it, and I've got to save my skin."

She knew that Paul was desperate and terribly frightened, and that it was only the dope which he had already taken which was keeping him at all sensible and capable of going on.

The pupils of his eyes were dilated and he was very white, but he was in the frame of mind when he would stick at nothing to get his own way.

Metaphorically, Fiona shrugged her shoulders.

There was nothing to be done but to help him to escape, and whether she gave him the money pleasantly, or made a scene about it, the results would be exactly the same.

"Come on, now," said Paul, "I'd better be getting on with it. If you give me away, the moment I've gone, Fiona, I'll get even with you. I'll drag you into this, and say you were my accomplice."

"I won't give you away," Fiona answered quietly.

But Paul was in too mad a frame of mind to be appeased by her gentleness.

"You'd better not!" he said quickly. "Come on—"

She turned out the light and stepped into the silent passage.

They went down about three floors, and then very cautiously drew up the blind of the landing window.

As Fiona had said, the fire-escape ran straight down

the side of the house into the yard. Beyond the yard was a mews, but it was impossible to say from where they were if there was anybody waiting there or not.

As silently as they could—but Fiona felt that her heart was beating so loud that everyone would wake and hear it—they opened the window, and as soon as he could Paul squeezed himself out on to the fire-escape.

Then without a word and in complete silence, he crept down the iron steps.

Very gently Fiona shut the window behind him, and then put her face close to the pane so as to be able to see what happened to him.

He got to the end of the iron stairs, and she saw him bend down, clutch the bottom rail with his hands and swing free for one agonising moment.

Then he dropped, and for a second she thought how awful it would be if he had broken his leg, and she had to explain how he had left her, and what part she played in his escape. But he was all right.

She saw him pick himself up and creep silently across the little yard, which was used only to reach the coal cellar, the tradesmen's entrance being, as Fiona had said, in the basement in the front of the house.

Fiona felt sure that the yard door into the mews would be locked, but apparently it was only bolted from the inside. She watched Paul draw back the bolt and very cautiously open the door.

He peered through a small crack, and then, reassured, opened it a fraction wider.

He put his head outside and glanced quickly from right to left, and seeing nothing, he stepped through, closing the door behind him, and vanished.

Fiona drew down the blind and crept upstairs. Only when she regained her bedroom did she realise how much she was shaking and how cold she was, with fright and the chilliness of the evening.

She huddled down before the electric fire, holding out her hands to its warmth, and then she saw her jewel-case and remembered how little it contained.

155

Five pounds—and to-morrow she had to start again looking for a job! She put her face between her hands, and slow tears came to her eyes.

She was not crying from bitterness and misery, but from sheer discouragement.

The next morning she was subjected to strenuous examination at the police station.

It seemed to her they kept her there for hours, questioning her over and over again, but finally her frank and—in most cases—truthful answers convinced them and they let her go.

They had nothing against her, but she felt that for some time to come she would be kept in all probability under their observation.

She wondered as she left the police station where she might be likely to obtain another job. She was tired out, for she had little sleep the night before, and the shock had told on her more than she realised at first.

Impelled by a weariness that would not be denied, she went home to go to bed.

As Fiona got into the lift and it slowly climbed the floors to her room, she felt a fear of the future grip her.

What did it hold for her in the days to come? What would happen to her, now that she was once again penniless and alone?

She knew that she could not let Donald know that she was penniless and really in need of the money he had borrowed from her.

While she had been working in the last few months she had meant to ring him up and speak to him, but somehow the days had passed by.

She had always been too tired, or too busy, and now that she was again without money and without work, she knew that she could not disturb Donald's peace of mind by letting him know.

However, five pounds would carry her on a little way.

She had given provisional notice to leave her room at the end of the week, reserving the option of staying on

should she in the meantime find a job which would en-
able her to pay for it.

"I've always been lucky before," she thought; "perhaps I shall be lucky now."

CHAPTER SEVEN

The streets were wet, and there was a promise of further rain in the dark, lowering sky, which hung grey and moist over the house-tops.

Fiona stood on the steps of the boarding-house where she had spent the night for two shillings, and wondered which way she would turn.

It was February—nearly two months since Fiona had been in work, and already the life she was leading, of hunger and hopeless searching, had altered her almost out of all recognition.

She was very thin, and the black coat which had fitted her so snugly now hung in ungainly folds over her hips and from her thin shoulders.

It was worn at the cuffs, and almost threadbare where she had held it across her to keep out the bitter east winds. She had worn it for twelve hours of the day, for by now she had nothing else left to wear.

All her other clothes had gone their way one by one, to the pawnbrokers, who had begun to greet her with friendly nods and a cheerful word, as she entered their dingy precincts.

She had moved from room to room, becoming poorer and poorer, until finally she had spent last night in a boarding-house in Charing Cross Road, where she had shared a bedroom with two other women.

She had been almost too frightened to creep between the dirty sheets, grey and discoloured, which had obviously not been changed for some weeks.

She had been too nervous to ask the other occupants —a blowsy woman of fifty with a penchant for gin, and a thin, emaciated girl with a consumptive cough—if she might have the window open.

They had stared at her in hostile silence as she had entered the room, the last comer.

They had watched her half undress, disdaining to address any remark but obviously suspicious of her good underclothes, and scornful of the trouble she took to wash in the cold water provided in a tin basin.

After that, her suitcase had to go to the pawnbroker's, and the two shillings she had spent last night had been almost all that she possessed in the world.

She had exactly threepence-halfpenny in her bag, and with this she hoped to get herself some food for the day.

She realised, as she went down the street, that she was desperately hungry, and knew by the lightness of her head that she could not go without food for much longer.

Twice she had nearly fainted lately, and once a kindly policeman had helped her from the ground into a side street, where she could recover.

There was a cheap eating-house she knew of in a squalid street off Shaftesbury Avenue, and she walked in there now, the wet soaking through her thin shoes so that she felt her feet becoming damp and cold.

The eating-house was small, but warm. Fiona sat down at a table which was already occupied by another girl, a rather pretty girl in a somewhat coarse manner, with thick lips and bold dark eyes.

She gave Fiona a flashing glance while she continued to eat a large sausage roll with evident enjoyment.

Fiona looked at the prices, and finally chose a sausage roll for twopence and a large slice of cake for threehalfpence.

So great was her hunger that she could hardly wait until the waitress brought them, and when they were at last before her she started to eat them almost ferociously.

159

The girl opposite looked up with a smile.

"You seem hungry," she said.

"I am," Fiona confessed, almost shamefacedly, knowing that she had seized upon her food in an uncontrolled manner.

The girl laughed.

"I know," she said, "I've felt like it myself. Going to have a cup of coffee?"

Fiona shook her head.

"This is my last halfpenny," she said.

The girl looked sympathetic.

"Have a cup with me," she said, "I can stand it—I'm in luck. I've just got a job."

Fiona accepted gratefully—she had no pride left where food and drink were concerned.

"What have you got?" she asked, when the coffee had been brought.

"I've got into the dance hall round the corner," the girl replied. "Night club, they call it, but I don't think there's much club about it. Anyone who pays can get in."

"Have they got any more vacancies?" Fiona asked wistfully.

Her new-found friend looked at her.

"D'you dance?" she said. "You're pretty, if you didn't look so pinched."

Fiona nodded.

"I always have been in a club," she said. "I was at the New Broadway Club for four months."

The girl seemed to consider.

"The New Broadway—I don't think I've heard about that one. What happened to it?"

"It got closed up," Fiona replied; "the manager was arrested for dope traffic."

"Oh yes, I remember—it was very classy, wasn't it?"

Fiona nodded.

"Haven't you had a job since?" she was asked.

She shook her head.

"I've just about come to the end," she said. "I've sold everything I can."

"You oughtn't to have any trouble in getting off," her friend replied, but Fiona shook her head.

"That's not my style," she said, and the girl gave a snort.

"Beggars can't be choosers," she replied almost angrily, as if Fiona had reproached her.

"Please tell me about this club," Fiona begged. "Do you think I could get into it?"

"Well, I don't know," the girl answered. "We could go along and see. She's choosing them this morning. I came along early, and got picked out at once. Anyhow, it can't do any harm. It's only round the corner, I'll take you—come on."

"Will you really?" Fiona said. "It's most awfully kind of you!"

"Half a mo," her friend said, "you'd better make your face up a bit more."

Over the table she offered Fiona her rouge and lipstick, and Fiona gratefully made up her face at the small mirror in her handbag.

Finally, feeling better for the food inside her, and her war-paint well adjusted, she walked across the road with her new friend.

Gladys Truson, she discovered, had been born in the Old Kent Road. Her mother was a washer-woman, and had already brought into the world six other children.

She meant well. She was extremely generous to her companions, she was good company; she was young and for the moment comparatively fresh-looking.

Gladys was certainly enjoying the present, though what the future held for her she at least had no idea.

She took Fiona now to a rather dirty-looking house in a narrow and, at night, very dimly lighted street. The door was open, and the stairs, uncarpeted, led twisting and narrow to the basement.

Here, to Fiona's surprise, was a large-sized room, quite amusingly decorated.

It had a good floor and a bandstand at one corner; looking-glasses and red plush sofas predominated, while at one end was a large bar, at the moment shuttered and locked.

In the centre of the floor, a small, fat woman was talking to several smartly dressed girls, who were giggling before her.

"And mind, girls," she was saying, "I don't want any of you wasting your time on beer men. What I say is, if they can't have champagne when you're out on a jaunt, when the devil are they going to have champagne?

"If they can't afford champagne, then they needn't come here, taking up the places of those who can."

She broke off speaking as Gladys and Fiona advanced across the polished floor towards her.

"Hullo, you!" she said to Gladys. "What do you mean by running off before I had a talk with you? You'd better come and listen to what I'm saying.

"And who's this?" she said, pointing at Fiona. "We don't want any more here."

"This is a friend of mine," Gladys said eagerly. "Do take her on—she's had a heap of experience. She was at the New Broadway Club with all the nobs, and she can dance like an angel—can't you, Fiona?"

The woman snorted.

"We don't want any angels here," she said, but she was obviously impressed by Fiona's graceful air and general appearance.

It was quite plain that she was of a far better type than the other girls who were hanging round listening to this conversation.

Fiona, with her fairness and somewhat fragile air, looked like a creature from another world.

"Take your hat off!" she was commanded, and as she pulled off her close-fitting beret her hair, untouched by peroxide, fell out in its thick waves and stood round her thin face like a pale halo.

"H'm, not bad," the woman said. "I suppose I shall have to take her. Do you know the terms?"

Fiona nearly leapt with joy. A job—she'd got it!

What did it matter what the terms were? She supposed there would be tips.

"Five bob a week," she was told, "and sandwiches if you want them."

She was only too pleased to accept, and then, as she agreed gratefully, she remembered that she had no evening dress.

After a few more bright remarks to the girls, "Ma," as she was called by the girls, told them to skip off and to be back again sharp at ten o'clock.

Outside the club, Fiona put her arm through Gladys's.

"I can't thank you enough," she said. "I am most terribly grateful. You really have saved my life!"

"Oh, go on!" Gladys said, almost embarrassed by Fiona's sincere tone. "You'd have got something, but still I'm glad you're coming with me. We'll have rather fun together."

"There's one thing," Fiona said, "I haven't got a dress. Do you know anywhere round here where I could get one on tick? Or else I could leave my coat in exchange."

Gladys appeared to consider.

"I think I could fix you up to-night," she said. "With any luck, you'll get enough tips in two or three nights to buy one."

"Can you really?" Fiona said. "How terribly kind you are!"

"Come on—let's go and try it on," Gladys said.

They went up the Tottenham Court Road and turned down a small side street. Gladys let herself in at the door of a dirty, dilapidated house which had obviously seen better days and was badly in need of a coat of paint, and Fiona had never in her life seen such an untidy room as Gladys's.

Everywhere there were pieces of paper, dirty bits of cloth, old ribbons, underclothes, a half-eaten bun; the dressing-table was a mess of dirty, dusty pots and used bits of cotton-wool, an old powder-puff, and a hair-brush almost bare of bristles and covered with dusty hairs.

From behind the door, hanging on a peg, Gladys produced three dresses.

"I think I'll wear my white one to-night," she said, holding up a wisp of chiffon which could very well have done with a clean.

"I've got a new sash for it that I brought in the sales, and a little sequin coat, and it looks a dream. Which would you like? This red—which has got a bit stained —or do you prefer the black?"

Fiona chose the black, which was of a cheap lace, and though torn and damaged where Gladys had put her foot through the flounces and torn it under the arm, it was quiet and unpretentious.

"Have you got a needle and cotton?" she asked, and after a prolonged hunt Gladys managed to find some black cotton, but no needle.

"Wait a minute, I'll borrow one from the front room," she said.

For the next hour, Fiona laboriously mended and patched the black lace dress ready for that evening's entertainment.

*　　*　　*

The "Flashlight Club" did not start to be really entertaining until well on into the early hours of the morning.

Nevertheless, the girls were supposed to be there by ten o'clock.

Fiona, arriving with Gladys, was introduced all round, but after a "pleased to meet you," the girls did not address much of their conversation to her.

This was not inhospitality, but merely due to the fact that their conversation consisted almost entirely of a running commentary on the people they all knew, and a somewhat frank confessional of their doings since they last met.

They all seemed to be old hands at the game, with the exception of one dark-skinned little French girl, who had obviously been engaged for her outstanding looks.

The rest had served under "Ma" before—who, Fiona gathered, was in the habit of opening night club after night club, and moving to a new one each time the police shut her down.

"Ma" was evidently quite a good sort, but it was wise to keep on the right side of her.

Once she banned a girl from her clubs, it was impossible to get back. However, she meant to work them hard, and she did, as Fiona found later in the evening.

No girl was allowed to remain without a partner. Either "Ma" brought one up to her, or else she was told to "see about one—and damn quick, too!"

About eleven-thirty, a few clients arrived, young men slightly the worse for drink.

Most of these were greeted affectionately by their Christian names by the girls, who hung on to their arms, talking and laughing and persuading them to stand drinks all round.

By twelve o'clock the place was nearly full. Fiona found herself dancing with one man after another.

Before they came, Fiona had asked Gladys what she was to do about a room for the night.

"I have no money," she said. "Do you think your landlady would let me have one on tick?"

Gladys looked doubtful.

"I don't know," she said.

Then she had an idea.

"I tell you what, you can sleep with me if you like to-night—that is, if I'm not busy. If I am, I'll find you somewhere outside. If I'm not, well, it's okay. It's open night, so unless I get a boy that I've known before I'm not likely to find a new boy.

"They generally come once or twice and get pally. That is, unless he's a 'Bond-streeter.' "

"What's a Bond-streeter?" Fiona asked interestedly.

"Ships that pass in one night," said Gladys.

They then sounded the landlady, who admitted that

she had a bed in the attic which could be had for half a crown, if desired.

Gladys did not tell her that she was asking for this information on Fiona's account, but merely said she had a friend coming up from the country who might require a room.

The landlady, however, was not taken in by this guileless story.

"That's all right," she said, "I know your games. Your friend will be sleeping with you if you haven't got anyone better.

"All right, make your own arrangements, but let me warn you that if there's been so much as a finger laid on that bed in the morning, I have my half-crown—or out you both go."

At three o'clock the Flashlight Club was a riot of gaiety. Coloured lights revolved on the walls, changing the dancer's faces from heliotrope to green, from green to orange, and back to purple.

The band made more noise than Fiona had imagined it possible for any jazz-band to make, the reason being that the ceiling was low and there was no escape for the sound.

However, the blatant melody seemed to incite the dancers to further hilarity.

The bar was doing a roaring trade, which, apart from anything else, was not surprising, owing to the almost suffocating heat of the room.

The dancers seemed quite unaffected by the atmosphere. They danced on and on, more and more vigorously, until Fiona, who was not in a fit state to stand much exercise, felt that she must drop on the floor if she did not rest.

There was no high tipping here, and it was impossible to insist that any man should tip the girl he danced with.

It was an understood thing, but at the same time Fiona found now and then that many men were shirkers, unless the girl was persistent.

Fiona found it almost impossible to insist, as some

of the girls did, on a larger tip, though many got it because their partners would rather pay than have a scene.

In some cases, a man would ask a girl to go home with him, and if she refused would drop her disdainfully, without a tip, even if he had monopolised her for two or three dances before he made up his mind.

For this there was no redress, as the girls themselves considered it silly not to accept a man who offered enough, and "Ma" would have been furious had she known that her customers were being disappointed.

It was five o'clock when Fiona and Gladys finally left, although Fiona had not seen Gladys for some hours during the evening, and wondered what had happened to her.

However, when closing time came she was hanging around with the others, all rather tired and dishevelled.

They swung along at a brisk rate up the Tottenham Court Road towards the house. Fiona's feet were aching, and there was a large blister on her heel.

Nevertheless, she knew she had over ten-shillings-worth of silver in her bag, and this at the moment was worth all the tiredness in the world.

"I think I'll have that bed to-night," she said to Gladys. "I need a good rest."

"You'll need your money to-morrow," Gladys said. "Don't be a fool—if you get a friendly offer you'd much better take it."

"I know, I need a dress too," Fiona answered. "I can't be grateful enough for what you have done for me, Gladys."

"Oh, shut up!" Gladys answered, as they arrived at their door and tiptoed into the house.

Gladys's room was more messy and untidy than ever. The bed was tumbled and bits of clothing were lying all over the place.

Fiona felt a great distaste at having to sleep there, but at the same time she knew that she must try and get herself an evening dress as quickly as possible, so as not to continue wearing Gladys's.

There was nothing else for it, and tired, but still laughing at their jokes, the two girls got into bed together.

*　　*　　*

Three weeks later, Fiona was an old hand at the "Flashlight." She soon found her feet, learned to call most of the habitués by their Christian names, and also became more or less proficient at demanding higher tips without appearing to do so.

It was a noisy, rather strenuous life, for there were continual rows. The sordidness of the place was at its most apparent on Saturday nights.

Then the proceedings nearly always managed to get rough, and the people who came always seemed to Fiona to be a worse class than on any other night.

A lot of them, however, were couples, who only wanted to dance together, but Fiona dreaded the time when a dozen or so youths would come on after some dinner or festive occasion.

Then, already the worse for drink, they made the place into a kind of bear-garden, upsetting the other clients, and being on more than one occasion so rough that the girls got knocked about.

Fiona herself, having been knocked down in a scuffle on the floor, had a bruise on her legs which was extremely painful, and one girl got her head cut open by a broken glass.

Ma seemed to consider this all in the day's work, and indeed, from her point of view, Saturday night, though troublesome to manage, was the best night of all, for the takings nearly always exceeded any other evening.

Then one night things went too far.

There had been some football club celebration, and a large number of members, already in an advanced state of intoxication, arrived at the "Flashlight" about 12.30, presumably when other places were closing their bars.

168

They rushed to the "Flashlight" bar as soon as they arrived, and were there sometimes, drinking, shouting and singing songs, but otherwise in nobody's way.

The dance floor was very crowded. There had been a wedding in the neighbourhood, and the best man and ushers had brought a party which included some of their own women.

One or two of the men danced with the dance-hostesses, as the party had several men too many, but the girls were not asked to join their table, being returned to their own corner as the dance ended.

Presently one of the football team moved from the bar on to the dancing floor.

Choosing a girl from the wedding party who was already dancing, he "cut in."

Her partner expostulated angrily, but he ignored him, pulling the girl all the time towards him on the dance-floor.

Amid shouts and ejaculations, and a scream from the girl, the man hit him, and the football player crashed against a table which was covered with glasses.

After that there was pandemonium. Everyone seemed to be fighting everyone else.

The football team, in their enthusiasm to help their friend, laid out a few strangers. The noise was terrific, women screaming, men shouting.

Ma and Joe and the barman rushed backwards and forwards, shouting instructions, striving by battering on the fighting backs nearest to them to quell the tumult, but their voices were lost and no one listened.

Fiona found herself huddled in a corner of the room with two other girls, trying to get a small sofa between them and the mob which kept swaying towards them, knocking over chairs and tables.

Suddenly down the stairs came several policemen.

The arm of the law sternly but indomitably cleared the room in no time.

Two or three men were arrested, and one man, who was badly battered, was carried upstairs and taken away later in an ambulance.

169

The police were accompanied in their work by Ma, chattering cheerily, explaining, remonstrating, but they took no notice of her.

Finally, when the hall was cleared, the girls, like Fiona, who had evidently taken no part in the show, were taken off to the police station.

Gladys shrugged her shoulders as they stepped out into the drizzling rain.

"It would rain!" she said crossly. "I don't know how you feel, Fiona, but I don't think it's worth taking a cab. You're out of work again, my dear."

"Do you mean to say the club will not be open to-morrow night?" Fiona asked anxiously.

"Of course I do," Gladys answered. "You don't suppose they'll let her go on running it with all that drink after hours? She'll do another stretch before she starts again."

"How long will she get?" asked Fiona curiously.

"About six months, I should think," Gladys replied. "This will be her third or fourth conviction."

In depressed silence they walked the rest of the way, the damp soaking into their thin satin slippers and the rain taking the last remnant of wave from Gladys's hair.

"Gawd, what a life!" said the latter, as they reached home. "You'd better share my room to-night, Fiona. That'll save you two-and-a-tanner."

Fiona thankfully agreed, the terror of the morrow taking her once again into its powerful grip.

* * *

Within a week Fiona was once again down to her last sixpence.

Gladys was also hard up, but at the same time she made enough to pay her rent by going out in the evening on the only errand on which Fiona would not accompany her.

"I can't, Gladys . . . I just can't," she said when her friend expostulated. "I'd rather starve."

"Just because you were once in love with a chap you don't see now, I can't see the point in letting yourself die," Gladys said. "You'll come to it in the end, when you are too down and out to care and not in a position to bargain. I think you're a fool."

In view of her friend's opinion, Fiona had not told her that she had lately come down to her last sixpence.

For the two previous nights, Gladys had wanted her bedroom, and Fiona had been forced to pay for the room at the top of the house.

Although the landlady had come down to two shillings, she would not let it any cheaper.

Fiona had begged her to take less, but she had remained adamant, turning a deaf ear to her pleadings.

To-night Fiona realised she could not sleep there, and once again she had refused Gladys's offer to accompany her to the Tottenham Court Road and on to Shaftesbury Avenue.

She thought if she walked until four or five in the morning Gladys would then very likely be alone, and she could creep into her room and shelter there the remaining hours of the night.

Everything she possessed had been pawned already, even down to her last decent set of underclothes, and as she wandered out now the evening air struck chill against the very poor resistance of her thin coat and the chiffon dress she wore under it.

She sauntered down the road looking into the shops and wondering how she could kill time until four o'clock.

It was only nine now, and she had no money to spend on food, although she promised herself a cup of coffee later in the evening.

An hour later she found herself on the Embankment. She wandered along aimlessly, hoping she might find a seat on which she could rest, but these were all occupied by shapeless bundles of humanity striving to snatch a little sleep.

It started to rain, at first only a misty drizzle, turning

171

later into a hard downpour. Fiona tried to find shelter in an Underground station, but without avail.

She was moved on, and after walking Citywards, she turned down one of the unfrequented streets at the back of a huge warehouse.

At the end of this a short arch spanned the very narrow roadway, and under this she had a little shelter.

It was almost dark here. The street lamps were few and far between, there being no traffic at night and the warehouses around being barred and closed until the morning.

She stood shivering against the cold stone, hoping the rain would soon abate and she could wander back towards a more lighted spot. It was lonely here, and she felt small and crushed by circumstances.

What years ago it seemed since she had stood on the balcony of the Careys' house, under the stars, feeling then that she was insignificant and inconspicuous—that night in which she had told Jim of her love and knew that no other man could ever matter in her life.

As she looked back at the past months, she thought of the men who had asked her for favours which she had refused.

Strangely enough, none of them seemed to stand out vividly in her mind. She wondered if she would be able to recognise them again, and decided she would not.

It was easier to remember the men who laughed and danced with her and stood her drinks good-humouredly, than those who had asked for more.

The moment she had realised, when dancing with them, that they desired more than an hour's jolly companionship, she had instinctively dismissed them from her mind as quickly as she had dismissed them from her side.

No man should hurt the love that whatever happened to her, was Jim's for ever.

"Whatever happens to me" she repeated to herself—and wondered how soon anything would!

Through the rain, which was coming down in a sharp, steady stream as though it meant to continue for some time, she heard steps approaching, and round the corner came a shuffling dark figure.

Fiona shrank further against the wall. Like herself, it was a poor bit of humanity seeking shelter, a man whose clothes betrayed him as a real down-and-out.

He stopped under shelter a few feet away from Fiona, and peered at her from under a dripping and torn cap.

He stood for a moment looking at her, then shuffled a little nearer along the wall.

"Got any money?" he said at last, in a hoarse voice.

"No," Fiona answered quaveringly.

She was a little frightened.

This back street was very lonely, one could hardly hear the traffic, and the only sound was the noise of of the rain.

"Yer must have somethin'," the hoarse voice said.

"I've got nothing," Fiona said sharply, edging a little way along the wall.

Then she gave a terrified shriek, for a claw-like hand came from out of the bundle of ragged clothes and snatched at her arm.

She pulled her arm away, but the hand caught at her bag, and as she held on to it the handle snapped and slithered through her grasp. In her fright, she turned and fled into the rain, too scared to argue, too fearful to call a policeman.

There was only sixpence in her bag, but it also held her powder-puff and last few personal objects.

Dreadful tales of what had happened to girls down by the river flashed into her mind, and she ran as hard as she could.

She slipped on the wet pavement but too anxious to get away to care, until once again she was under the lights of populous thoroughfare.

The rain rapidly soaked her to the skin. She could feel little rivulets trickling down her neck and down her cold cheeks.

She splashed along, trying here and there to find

shelter, obtaining perhaps a minute or two's respite but always turned away.

A policeman moved her on kindly but firmly from the doorway of a large building, and she was too frightened to seek again the side turnings, where in the darkness of the Adelphi Arches she might have found temporary protection.

She walked the length of the Embankment, until she came to the Houses of Parliament. Here she turned right, and made her way again to Trafalgar Square.

A coffee stall, with its appetising piles of rolls and pies, was serving a crowd of taxi-drivers.

Fiona hesitated for some time within radius of its warm, inviting hospitality. She wished she had the sixpence which had been stolen from her.

She remembered that Gladys had told her that no woman was served late in the evening if she was alone, that one had to be accompanied by a man.

What harm there was in selling a lonely woman a cup of coffee, Fiona could not understand, but the laws of England were apparently intended to discourage any woman, whatever her age, from being abroad at night.

A taxi-driver, seeing her hesitating, said to her kindly:

"Want a coffee, Miss? I'll ask for you."

Fiona shook her head.

"Haven't got any money, thanks," she replied.

"Hard luck," he growled, and went on to order his own needs.

Slowly Fiona walked away. An hour later, she was still walking. She had looked at the clock—it was only a quarter to one. Not time to return.

Three and a quarter more hours before she dare. She was so wet and so cold that somehow she had ceased to notice it.

She just felt numb, her legs moved automatically, and although once or twice she was attacked by fits of shivering and her teeth chattered, they passed off, and she just moved onwards and onwards.

Where could she go, what could she do? She walked

174

and walked, and suddenly she had a desire to look at the flat where she and Jim had been so happy.

She turned her weary footsteps, and somehow at her thought, some of her weariness seemed to vanish. Her teeth had ceased to chatter, but she felt strangely light-headed and in a sort of daze.

Her cheeks, down which the rain was trickling, were now burning.

Her body felt almost as though it did not belong to her, her hands, purple and pinched, held her soaking coat around her.

It dragged against her wet stockings, chafing the flesh underneath, but she did not notice it. On she walked, talking to herself.

Once or twice she met people who hurried past her. Her hair hung in damp streaks against her cheeks, her hat, soaked out of recognition, was pushed back on her head.

Only her eyes, wide and dark, were unchanged, seeming to look forwards and onwards, seeing things which were frightening in the dark, rain-washed world of reality.

Past Hyde Park Corner, up Park Lane—she knew where she turned, and there before her was the block of flats, the door she had entered so often, the windows of the flats above.

Could she remember which window had been hers? She craned her neck, but somehow could not see.

"Jim!" she kept saying to herself, "This is where Jim lived. Fiona lived there, Fiona and Jim."

She murmured the names over and over again, and then crept nearer to the doorway.

If only she had the latchkey . . . if only she could enter now, go up to her little flat. Fiona and Jim! . . . that was where they had lived.

Suddenly she was terror-stricken, her hands were shaking, her teeth were chattering again.

"Fiona," she called faintly, "where is Fiona? . . . What has happened to her?"

175

She rushed frantically to the door and battered on it with her hands, and then, calling as in a frenzy.

"Let me in! Let me in! I must . . . find . . . Fiona!"

She pressed the bell at the side.

"Where's Fiona?" she called again, "where's Fiona?"

Suddenly the blackness seemed to envelop her. She put out her hands and found no support, she was going, drifting down into a darkness which was overwhelming.

"Fiona!" she cried again, "where . . . is Fiona?"

She fell senseless on the white marble steps.

CHAPTER EIGHT

Jim was sitting in front of the fire in his flat in Portland Place. He had dined alone, and was now smoking a cigar.

He was much older-looking than a year before. There were lines on his forehead and round his eyes that had not been there in the days when he and Fiona had laughed so happily together.

There was even a suspicion of grey hairs just over his ears, and his expression was one of intense seriousness as he stared at the bright flames which were eating up the big log laid across them.

The clock struck ten, and he rang the bell for his servant.

"Bring the drinks," he said when the man appeared. "I am expecting Dr. Morton shortly, and after that I shall not require you any more."

"Very good, sir."

The man brought in a small table and a moment later appeared with a silver tray heavily laden with decanters and a plate of sandwiches.

"Will you be called at the usual time, sir?" he asked, and Jim nodded his head.

"I'll ride, as usual," he replied.

Alone, Jim got to his feet and walked slowly up and down. Something was troubling him greatly, something requiring thought and concentration.

At last he sat down again and waited, his eyes on the

clock. A few minutes later, the door was opened and Dr. Morton was announced.

A short, grave man, with grey hair, he entered, hurriedly pulling off a large pair of driving gloves, handing these a moment later, with a fur-lined overcoat, to the waiting servant.

"I'm sorry to be late," he said. "I had to call in at home on the way, for several messages, otherwise I should have been here before. May I help myself to a drink?"

Jim nodded, and the doctor helped himself to a mild whisky and soda, and took a sandwich.

"Well?" Jim said at last.

The doctor shook his head.

"No hope, I'm afraid. Sir Barnaby examined her thoroughly."

"Will he operate?" Jim asked.

Dr. Morton shook his head again.

"I'm afraid not," he said. "It has gone too far. I informed Sir Barnaby that you had refused us any family details until after the examination, but I expect you can very likely now throw some light on the subject."

Jim walked to a far corner of the room and stood for a moment looking at the doctor.

"First of all," he said, "am I right in thinking that Sir Barnaby's verdict is the same as yours—that my wife is incurably insane?"

"She has a very enlarged brain tumour," Dr. Morton replied.

He put a hand on Jim's shoulder.

"I hated to bring this verdict," he said. "It is unlikely she will live for more than three months. It might be sooner."

Jim sighed and sat down in a chair.

"You have been very kind," he said; "I can't attempt to thank you."

"Don't try," the doctor answered. "One thing we never expect in our profession is thanks. The only

178

thing I would like would be to hear the story of the case."

He settled himself opposite Jim, and took a cigar from the box offered him.

After a few silent moments, Jim started to speak. His voice was deep and at times broke a little, his face was intensely serious and he chose his words with care.

"When I first met my wife," he said, "the thing that attracted me to her was not only her beauty but also the fact that I considered she was being abominably treated by her first husband.

"He always spoke to her as if she were an irresponsible child, or someone not responsible for her actions. I was incensed by this, and that, if nothing else, spurred me on to make love to her.

"She became attached to me, and later obtained a divorce from her husband, not bringing me into it—in fact, I didn't know such an action was to be brought until it was completed.

"I knew nothing of her family, and very little about her. I never saw her until her decree was made absolute, and then she came to London and we met after a separation of nearly a year.

"I must say this now, because it has some little bearing on the story, but during the time I had been apart from Ann I had realised that my feelings for her were a mere passing infatuation.

"I was not really in love with her, although I only found this out through falling deeply in love with someone else. However, circumstances arranged that by the time Ann arrived in London, I was a free man in every sense of the word, although it was not within my power to make myself love her.

"She came to me excited and thrilled with her divorce. She was very beautiful, and yet her beauty left me cold.

"There was something a little hysterical about her greeting of me, something a little over-excited and too exuberant about her feelings, which she expressed very forcibly.

"I thought at the time that I was over-critical, perhaps

179

unjust to her, and I strove to make myself as pleasant as possible.

"We arranged to be married within a few weeks' time, and it was then I suggested she should introduce me to her family.

" 'They are abroad,' she said, 'living abroad. I never see them.'

"She looked queerly at me as she said it, and somehow I had the impression that she was lying, though I could imagine no conceivable reason why she should not wish me to meet them.

"Finally, as she had no relations to produce, I took her round to meet mine, who were all delighted with her beauty and charm. There was only one incident which has any bearing on the story.

"I took Ann to meet my uncle, an old man who spends most of his time now at his club, but who in his day was a famous Master of Hounds.

"I mentioned that Ann had lived in Leicestershire, and he at once pricked up his ears and asked her if she hunted.

"She said no, and I myself supplied the information that her first husband had been a hard rider to hounds. My uncle at once connected the name with that of man he had met some years previously.

" 'It can't be the same, however,' he said finally; 'the man I knew made a most unfortunate marriage with a girl whose family were notorious in Somerset.'

"To my surprise, as he spoke Ann sprang to her feet, and said we must be going. She pleaded another appointment, and almost ran me out of the house.

"At the time, I thought nothing of it, and then, when it did cross my mind, I thought perhaps she was bored, or that she knew the story and it might in some way affect her as concerning her first husband, or his relations.

"In fact, it made very little impression on me at the time, although later I remembered the incident.

"We were married, as you know, at a register office, and went abroad to Monte Carlo for the honeymoon

From the very first, I'm afraid Ann was disappointed in me.

"God knows, Morton, that I am telling you the truth when I say that I tried to be a good husband to her, but it's hard for a man to be a good lover if his heart is not in it and try as I would I could not make myself have any real affection for Ann.

"There was something grasping, almost greedy, in the way she demanded my time, my love and my attention.

"She seemed to me to be snatching at me, to be frightened of missing something, to be greedily wanting to devour anything I could give her, and a good deal which I could not.

"Finally, one evening at Monte Carlo there was a scene. It all began over some quite trivial attention which I had failed to give her, and suddenly she had screaming hysterics.

"She screamed and sobbed until I was seriously alarmed, and sent for a doctor, who prescribed a soothing-draught and sent her to bed.

"That was the first of many scenes which for the next month or so were to make our life a complete hell. They got worse and worse.

"She would cry and yell until she was utterly exhausted, and then relapse into a kind of coma, almost an unconsciousness of anything around her.

"We came back to England, and by this time I was seriously alarmed at what was going on. As you know, shortly after our return I sent for you, and I knew that from the very beginning you took a serious view of these occurrences.

"She became insanely jealous. If I even spoke to the housemaid, she accused me of behaving in an improper fashion.

"If I took my hat off to an acquaintance in the street or bowed to a woman friend in a restaurant, she would begin to show signs of being seriously disturbed, and sooner or later would work herself up into one of her mad rages.

"It was all fantastic. When I went out with her, I almost used to pray that I should meet no one I knew.

"Afterwards she would be sorry, throwing her arms round my neck, apologising, making me say I forgave her, but at the same time she seemed to have very little knowledge of what she had or had not said or done.

"One day there was such a scene over some quite unimportant woman to whom I had been forced to speak, that when we reached home she tore off her clothes, tearing them into shreds as she did so, and smashing anything within reach.

"Quite frankly, I was horrified, disgusted, and at the same time terrified of what she would do next. That was the time I tried to get you on the telephone, but you were out at a case.

"I asked for your partner, but he was away, and finally your secretary gave me the name of a nearby man, and he came hurrying to my call.

"My wife was lying on the floor when he arrived; the storm, however, had already abated and she was gradually sinking into one of the comas which I knew so well.

"The floor was littered with the objects she had smashed, her hair was dishevelled and tousled, her face was tear-stained out of all recogniton of her usual beauty.

"The doctor and I finally got her into bed, and he gave her an injection to keep her quiet. When we had left her, he said to me:

" 'Is there insanity in your wife's family?'

"The words came like a thunderbolt. I must have had suspicions at some time that there was some sort of secret that my wife was determined to keep from me at all costs.

"I remembered how strangely her first husband had behaved to her, and the very next day I took the train to Leicestershire and sought him out. I arrived at his house in the late afternoon.

"He had just returned from a day's hunting, and was still in his pink coat, with his boots bespattered with mud. He greeted me cheerily, but when I told him on what errand I had come, he looked at me with a strange compassion.

" 'I was afraid that was the reason for your visit,' he said.

"He then told me briefly the position. He had married Ann, attracted—as I had been—by her loveliness.

"When he met her, she had been living with an old uncle in Somerset, who had hastened on the match, apparently delighted at the prospect of getting rid of his niece.

"It was only a week after they had been actually married that the bridegroom found out the truth—that Ann's father and mother were before they died, incurably insane.

"Ann had known all about this, and for her perfidy in the matter his love changed to dislike and disgust. She had been as ready as her uncle to trap him into marriage.

"One thing he determined—that though he could not now escape from her, he would never bring tainted children into the world.

" 'That is my story,' he finished. 'You can imagine that I was not sorry to find that Ann was anxious for a divorce. For years we had lived together in name only.

" 'Had I know Ann was going to marry you, I would have warned you—but she was too clever for that. She never gave me any suspicion that you were concerned in the case.

" 'I did not know that Ann would marry again until I saw the announcement of your wedding in the papers, and it was then too late.'

"I came back from that interview," Jim continued, "feeling like a man who had received a mortal blow. I knew then that Ann was doomed, as her relations had been.

"The quiet life she had led with her first husband, the lack of excitement and lack of any form of sexuality, had doubtless kept her quieter and more controlled than she would have been otherwise.

"The mere fact of being in love with me, and of our marriage, had upset her balance."

For a moment Jim put his hand before his eyes.

"I was determined you should not know the story before Sir Barnaby examined her," he went on. "I wanted to try every chance of saving her without the question of heredity prejudicing your judgment."

Dr. Morton rose to his feet.

"You have done all you could," he said.

"I think it will be better for you not to see her. She would not recognise you. She will not suffer and I only hope that later you yourself will find happiness."

He pressed Jim's shoulder.

"That is unlikely," Jim replied bitterly.

There was silence in the room, then the telephone bell rang.

*   *   *

"Jim . . . Jim . . . don't let him . . . don't let him touch me . . . You mustn't kiss . . . me . . . I . . . belong to Jim! . . . Andrew, Andrew, speak to me! . . . Andrew's dead, he's dead I tell you . . . my dear, dear friend! . . . Tell Jim to come at once, he must take me away . . . No, Jim's married, he can't come . . .

"Would you like to dance with me?—Oh, come on! I'll soon teach you . . . there, that's fine . . . Oh no, we don't have any pay, only our tips . . . Yes, that's all . . . if people are kind.

"Don't, Paul, don't . . . you can't take it all! Not all that . . . leave me just something . . . please, Paul! . . . Oh, God, I can't pay the rent . . . please help me to pay the rent. I must have money by to-morrow . . . let me find a job . . . please, God, let me find a job.

"No! . . . I've said no . . . I'm sorry, but I can't. No, not to-morrow night, either . . . All right . . . tell her if you like . . . No! . . . I'm sorry . . . I've said no . . .

"That's the flat . . . that's where I lived with Jim and where I was so happy . . . Jim's gone . . . and Fiona's gone . . . where's Fiona?

184

"My head . . . it feels so hot . . . what has happened? Oh, Jim . . . Jim . . . Jim . . .

The voice rambling on feverishly, ceased for a moment, and the Doctor put a hand on her pulse, glancing at the temperature chart that the Nurse held before him.

The room was very quiet. It had the same clean, antiseptic smell that all rooms have in nursing homes. The Nurse moved quietly, her starched apron rustling a little.

There was an almost imperceptible knock at the door.

"Sir Thomas," the Nurse said in a whisper to the Doctor by the bedside.

He nodded his head as a small, genial-looking man entered.

"I've only just got your message," he said in a low voice.

Then busied himself with the patient. It was nearly a quarter of an hour before he left the room, to find Jim waiting outside.

"The crisis should be in another three or four hours," he said.

Jim's expression asked his opinion better than any words could have done.

"Do you think she will live?"

Sir Thomas looked at him kindly.

"We are doing our best," he answered gravely, and hurried away.

Dr. Morton came out of the room a few moments later.

"You must keep calm, my dear boy," he said. "Sir Thomas will be back soon, and if he can't save her, no one can."

"If only I'd known—if only I could have found her sooner! To think that she was starving in London, a few streets away perhaps, and I didn't know it!

"If she hadn't gone back to our old flat and the caretaker hadn't recognised her, I might never have found her. Think of it, Morton—she might have died, and I would never have known it! I made every possible enquiry, but it was difficult.

"Of course I meant to settle money on her before I married Ann but I kept putting things off. Then I couldn't find her."

"We all make mistakes," the doctor said kindly.

"Morton, you must save her! I've got to give her a chance again to be happy. I've got to make up for all she's suffered. I realise now how true she has been to me and how little I have ever done in return."

"If it is humanly possible to save her, Sir Thomas will do it," the Doctor replied.

He returned to the sick-room.

Jim waited. The Nurse went in and out, and later another Nurse joined her.

An hour and a half passed before there were footsteps down the passage, and Sir Thomas, accompanied by an assistant, entered Fiona's room.

The door shut behind him, and afterwards there was a long silence.

*　　*　　*

Fiona opened her eyes slowly.

At first she could make out very little of the objects round her. She felt very weary. A figure moved, and a woman in white bent over her.

She felt a cup being held to her lips, and drank eagerly.

'I wonder where I am,' she thought listlessly, and fell asleep.

It seemed only a few minutes before she was again conscious. Voices were speaking.

"It's a miracle," one said. "She's out of danger now. You'd better tell that young man—he'll be off his head with joy."

She wondered vaguely who the young man was, and what miracle had been performed, and then she drifted away into a peaceful, grey world which seemed to be holding her firmly in its arms.

The mists gradually were clearing around her, she felt herself being buoyed up on them, but at the same time they were creeping away. Someone was holding her hand.

For a moment she imagined that she felt someone kiss it. Who could be kissing her hand, she wondered, and the thought of Jim came to her.

Kissing her hand! How often . . . the grey mist caught her again, and she drifted away.

* * *

There was sunshine trying to creep through the curtains. They were pale curtains, and they could not keep out the persistent sun.

She could see it from where she lay—little tiny yellow fingers creeping round the corners of the blind.

"Sunshine," she thought, and her brain was puzzled by it.

But it was raining—she had left a world of rain! Why was she here, in this bed?

She opened her eyes further, and made a movement with her hands. Instantly a Nurse came to her side.

"Would you like a drink?" she asked gently.

Fiona tried to shake her head.

"Where am I?" she asked.

She was surprised at the weakness of her voice, a mere hoarse whisper.

"You are in a nursing home," the Nurse answered. "It's quite all right—you're not to worry, we're all looking after you."

"A nursing home?" Fiona thought. "How can I have got here?"

Then a sudden thought struck her.

"I haven't got any money," she said quickly.

"That's quite all right," said the Nurse, smiling. "We shan't want you to pay anything."

As Fiona lay back and thought of this with astonishment, the Nurse returned to her seat by the fire. Nothing to pay!

Fiona pondered on this for some time. She could not be in a free hospital, she knew that because she was in a room by herself, and somehow, from what she could see of it, it all looked too expensive.

Too tired to worry further, she fell asleep again.

She felt stronger and better when she next awoke, and the first thing that greeted her eyes was a mass of pink roses on the table beside her bed.

"Roses!" she thought.

There came the memory of a bowl of them, pink and blooming, on the dressing-table of the flat, as she had left them and Jim, so long ago.

Jim! Instantly the image of him jumped to her mind, and suddenly her dreams of the past day seemed to return to her.

She had dreamed she had heard his voice, dreamed she had felt his lips against her hand. Still, it was only a dream . . . she had dreamed it, dreamed that she had heard Jim's voice saying,

"Darling—my darling!"

There had been other voices in those strange dreams of hers, voices which seemed to call her back from a misty land in which she was drifting.

They called her back to pain, dragging her from oblivion into a temporary consciousness that somewhere in her body were aches and agonies that she wished to escape.

And yet one of those voices had been persistently Jim's.

She had tried to escape the pain so as to be able to dream of him better, and yet with his voice had come pain, as if they were together part of the dream she desired.

"Jim," she said weakly now, as she had said it so often unconsciously in the hours gone by.

As she spoke, she heard a soft rustle, and the Nurse left the room.

Suddenly she opened her eyes again, and for a moment she thought she was indeed deep in her dreams.

There, standing beside her, so near that she could

have touched him, was Jim himself! She stared at him for a moment, and then whispered his name.

"Darling," he said gently, and took her hand in his.

She was amazed to see tears in his eyes. Her brain was struggling with the question of why was he here, but she could not ask it.

She could only dumbly hold on to his hand, trying to see every one of his beloved features.

He looked tired and worried, yet nevertheless she was close to her own Jim again.

"Get better quickly, Fiona," he murmured, "I want you, darling."

Suddenly his voice quivered and broke, and he bent his head, putting his lips against her hand.

She longed to lift her other hand and lay it against his hair, but she was too weak.

She could only stare at him wonderingly, surprised and shaken, yet with a strange happiness stirring in her heart.

Jim was here—everything must be all right!

She could not talk to him, and he said little or nothing more, just kissed her hand, and after a moment or two went away.

For a long time she lay, lulled by her strange new happiness, and then she fell asleep.

*　　*　　*

Sunshine—but this time unfettered by curtains. It sparkled on Fiona's fair hair as she lay against the white pillows and brought to her the feeling of warmth and happiness.

The Nurse finished tidying her bed, and smiled at her.

"You certainly are better this morning," she said. "If you go on like this you will make a record recovery which will be another feather in Sir Thomas's cap!"

"Will . . . Jim come to . . . see me to-day?" Fiona asked, and the Nurse smiled again.

"I shouldn't be surprised," she said. "He's been here

every day, and practically every hour, for the last three weeks."

"Have I been here . . . three weeks?" Fiona said, and the Nurse nodded.

Presently, when she was alone, she looked at the blue sky outside the window. Its pale spring brilliance seemed to hold a promise for her. Things were better, how she did not know, but they were.

Spring had come, and the winter was past. Jim was with her—how and why, again she did not know—but the fact was in itself all-important.

"Will he come and see me soon?" she wondered.

For the first time she glanced at herself in the hand-mirror. Her face was very pale, her eyes were enormous.

There was the dawn of hope in her expression, which was apparent even to herself. But she dare not think of it, dare not comtemplate anything beyond the fact that in a few minutes she would see Jim again.

She lay waiting for him, and yet when finally the door opened and he came in, she felt utterly unprepared.

He came quietly to her bedside and took her hand in his. Then, as their eyes met, he bent and kissed her very gently.

At his touch, the blood rushed to her face in a wave of crimson, and the eyes she raised to his held unshed tears.

Jim took both of her hands in his and held them very tightly.

Then he drew a deep breath, and spoke as if he were taking an oath.

"You are not allowed to talk much, my darling," he said, "and I am only permitted to stay a few minutes with you, but I want to tell you that, from now on, and for all time, you belong to me. Just that, and the fact that I love you, Fiona, my precious."

"Is . . . it really . . . you?"

"My own wonderful darling, get well quickly," Jim pleaded. "I want to take you away, to have you all to myself. One day very soon we will be married, until then

I will make you happy my poor little love, and I'll never lose you again."

The radiance in Fiona's eyes transformed her whole face.

She felt she must be dreaming.

Then Jim's lips very gently touched hers and she felt a little flickering flame of life come back into her body.

It was what she had longed for, and dreamed of—it was the ecstasy Jim always gave her, the rapture which made them one.

"Forgive me for failing you, my precious," Jim said brokenly. "Forgive me for letting you suffer. It was all my fault."

"It doesn't . . . matter . . . now," Fiona answered.

As she spoke she knew that what she said was true, the past was behind them and soon it would be forgotten.

It was the future that was important, a future that held Jim, a future where she could be his wife.

She didn't ask how it was possible, she only knew that he was with her, that they would be married and be complete.

It was so wonderful, that the room seemed golden with sunshine. She felt her heart dancing with the joy of it.

"I . . . love . . . you," she whispered and saw the happiness in his eyes.